# Ana Historic

# Ana Historic

Daphne Marlatt

ANANSI

First published in Canada in 1988 by Coach House Press.
Published in 1997 by House of Anansi Press Ltd.

This edition published in 2004 by
House of Anansi Press Inc.
110 Spadina Avenue, Suite 801
Toronto, ON, M5V 2K4
TEL 416-363-4343 FAX 416-363-1017
www.anansi.ca

Distributed in Canada by
HarperCollins Canada Ltd.
1995 Markham Road
Scarborough, ON, M1B 5M8
Toll free tel. 1-800-387-0117

Distributed in the United States by
Publishers Group West
1700 Fourth Street
Berkeley, CA 94710
Toll free tel. 1-800-788-3123

House of Anansi Press is committed to protecting our natural environment.
As part of our efforts, this book is printed on Rolland Enviro paper:
it contains 100% post-consumer recycled fibres, is acid-free,
and is processed chlorine-free.

10 09 08 07 06    5 6 7 8 9

LIBRARY AND ARCHIVES CANADA CATALOGUING IN PUBLICATION DATA

Matlatt, Daphne, 1942–
Ana historic

ISBN-13: 978-0-88784-590-1
ISBN-10: 0-88784-590-8

I. Title

PS8576.A74A8 1997    813'.54    C96-932429-7
PR199.3.M37A8 1997

Cover design: Bill Douglas at The Bang
Front cover photograph: Perry Low
Author Photograph: Bridget MacKenzie

 Canada Council
for the Arts

Conseil des Arts
du Canada

ONTARIO ARTS COUNCIL
CONSEIL DES ARTS DE L'ONTARIO

*We acknowledge for their financial support of our publishing program the Canada
Council for the Arts, the Ontario Arts Council, and the Government of Canada
through the Book Publishing Industry Development Program (BPIDP).*

Printed and bound in Canada

for Cheryl Sourkes

'The assemblage of facts in a tangle of hair.'

SUSAN GRIFFIN

Who's There? she was whispering. knock knock. in the dark. only it wasn't dark had woken her to her solitude, conscious alone in the night of his snoring more like snuffling dreaming elsewhere, burrowed into it, under the covers against her in animal sleep. he was dreaming without her in some place she had no access to and she was awake. now she would have to move, shift, legs aware of themselves and wanting out. a truck gearing down somewhere. the sound of a train, in some yard where men already up were working signals, levers, lamps. she turned the clock so she could see its blue digital light like some invented mineral glowing, radium 4:23. it was the sound of her own voice had woken her, heard like an echo asking,

who's there?

echoes from further back, her fear-defiant child voice carried still in her chest, stealing at night into the basement with the carving knife toward those wardrobes at the bottom of the staircase. wardrobes. wordrobes. warding off what? first the staircase with its star scrawled on the yellow wall and COMRADE, an illicit word never heard upstairs but known from Major Hoople's talk about those sleazy reds who were always infiltrating from some foreign underworld and threatening to get under or was it into the bed. nobody ever erased or painted over the scrawl and nobody seemed to see it but her, like some signal blinking every time she had to go downstairs with the knife. Comrade / would she really kill? she who was only a girl but even so the oldest in her family recently settled in cold-war Vancouver of the Fifties – a cold country, Canada, her mother said, people don't care. would she kill if she had to? after all she was responsible for her younger sisters

9

sleeping innocent above while she, their guardian on those nights (babysitter wasn't quite the word), conscious and awake, unable NOT to hear, tiptoed after those suspicious noises – what if he were hungry, starved even, and so desperately from outside he would kill to get what he wanted, as afraid even as she, to get what he needed, while she who had her needs met, secure (was she really?) in her parents' house, trembling and bare-armed (in nightie even), she was merely in his way – no, he was in the wrong if he were there at all he meant to do them harm, and she would resist, righteously. she stood in front of the darkest of the six-foot wardrobes, teak, too big to place upstairs, big enough to hide Frankenstein, stood feeling her fear, her desperate being up against it, that other breathing on the other side of the door she could almost hear, would take him by surprise, her only real weapon, kick it open flashlight weaving madly yelling (don't let me see! don't let me!)
Who's There?

empty. it always was. though every time she believed it might not be. relief, adrenalin shaking her legs. she had chosen the darkest first and must go to each in turn, confronting her fear (for what if he were there, in one of the others, waiting til she had her back turned, absorbed and vulnerable and never thinking he would leap on her from behind?). wishing, even, that what she knew could be there would be there and she be taken, lost, just to show them. who? her parents who went out leaving her alone to defend the house. her mother who ...

my mother (who) ... voice that carries through all rooms, imperative, imperious. don't be silly. soft breast under blue wool dressing gown, tea breath, warm touch ... gone. I-na (the long drawn calling out at night for a drink of water, one more story, one last hug, as i experimented with attracting your attention, Mum-my, Mom-eee, Mah-mee ...)

I-na, I-no-longer, i can't turn you into a story. there is this absence here, where the words stop. (and then i remember –

i was two perhaps, you told me often enough, hurry up Annie, we have to go now, while i went on playing, paying no attention, Annie, hurry up! i'm going now! playing with your attention, delaying, and then there was silence, the whole house filled with it. Mummy, i cried, Mummy? and you said in a low distant voice i didn't recognize (i did but i knew i wasn't meant to): your Mummy's gone. i burst into tears. don't be silly, darling, i'm here, you see how silly you are – as if *saying* it makes it so. but it does, it did. you had gone in the moment you thought to say it, separating yourself even as you stood there, making what wasn't, what couldn't be, suddenly real.

and now you've made your words come true, making it so by an act of will (despair). gone. locked up in a box. frozen in all the photographs Harald took. the worst is that you will never reappear with that ironic smile, don't be silly, darling. pulling through. the worst is that it's up to me to pull you through. this crumbling apart of words. 'true, real.' you who is you or me. she. a part struck off from me. apart. separated.

she, my Lost Girl, because i keep thinking, going back to that time with you (and why weren't there Lost Girls in Never-Never Land, only Lost Boys and Wendy who had to mother them all, mother or nurse – of course they fought the enemy, that's what boys did) and what i did when i was she who did not feel separated or split, her whole body trembling with one intent behind the knife. and it was defense (as they say in every war). no, it was trespassing across an old boundary, exposing my fear before it could paralyse me – before i would end up as girls were meant to be.

who did my Lost Girl think might be there in that house on the side of a mountain on the edge of a suburb surrounded by private laurels? what did she think would come staggering out of the woods? those woods men worked in, building powerlines and clearing land for subdivision. those woods the boys on the rest of the block had claimed as theirs.

except for that part directly behind the garden, that part she and her sisters called the Old Wood, moulted and softened with years of needle drift, tea brown, and the cedar stump hollow in the middle where they nestled in a womb, exchanging what if's, digging further with their fingers, sniffing the odour of tree matter become a stain upon their hands like dried blood.

what if the boys came down from their fort in the Green Wood with slingshots and air gun? would their own string bows and crookedly peeled arrows hold them off? standing on the rockery for practice, shooting at the bull's-eye in the field (a stone in an empty lot), she despaired of herself, her sister-archers, her camarades – their arrows fell off the string, plopped on the dirt like so many cowpies. who cares? they said. they hurt their thumbs, they got tired, they went off to read Little Lulu (not even Sheba, Queen of the Jungle). but what if the boys ... what if the men tried to bulldoze their woods? so what could *we* do? her little sister shrugged.

do, do. she my Lost Girl, my Heroine, wanted something to do not something that might be done to them. the refrain of a rainy afternoon: there's nothing to do! do something useful, her mother said, clean up your room. but she wanted out, in the fresh wet smell of cedar and rain.

tomboy, her mother said. tom, the male of the species plus boy. double masculine, as if girl were completely erased. a girl, especially a young girl, who behaves like a spirited boy – as if only boys could be spirited. who read Robin Hood, wore scarlet, identified with Lancelot and the boy who wanted to join the knights of St. John (all trespassers, law-breakers in the guise of saviours. what did 'useful' mean to them?)

the trouble was you gave me a sense of justice – your 'fair play,' Ina, your mother's instinct distributing things equally between us. but you would never admit it wasn't 'fair' that girls weren't allowed to do the things boys did. escape the house, 'home-free' – not home, but free in the woods to run, nameless in the split-second manoeuvre of deadfalls, bush blinds, ghost stumps glowing in the twilight. spirit(ed), filled with it, the world of what was other than us, tom as in thrum as in bullfrog sound, or the sudden awful drumming of a grouse.

it wasn't tom, or boy, it wasn't hoyden, minx, baggage, but what lay below names – barely even touched by them.

*'Douglas fir and red cedar are the principal trees. Of these, the former – named after David Douglas, a well-known botanist – is the staple timber of commerce. Average trees grow 150 feet high, clear of limbs, with a diameter of 5 to 6 feet. The wood has great strength and is*

13

*largely used for shipbuilding, bridge work, fencing, railway ties, and furniture. As a pulp-making tree the fir is valuable. Its bark makes a good fuel.'*

clear of limbs? of extras, of asides. tree as a straight line, a stick. there for the taking.

Mrs. Richards, who stood as straight as any tree (o that Victorian sensibility – backbone, Madam, backbone!) wasn't there for the taking. i imagine her standing slim in whalebone at the ship's rail as it turns with the wind, giving her her first view of what would become home as she imagined it, <u>imagining herself free of history.</u> (black poplin. useless baggage.) <u>there is a story here.</u>

## Arrival at Hastings Mill

She stood at the rail as the ship hove to, holding her bonnet against the wind and looking every inch a lady, lady-teacher that is, come to her first post. Would she look too young to them, too inexperienced for this outpost? – bush settlement, mill town (she would learn their terms, she would learn them as if from a book). Her dark skirt went suddenly slack in the loss of wind as they turned, edged by the tug in a slow momentum toward the wharf.

'Well, Mrs. Richards,' the captain's wife patted her hand, 'what do you think of your destination? A pretty harbour, is it not?'

14

She gazed at the piles of lumber, the heavy smoke, the low sprawling sheds. So many men, so foreign-looking, dressed in such an outlandish assortment of clothes. They were shouting to those on board in a great bustle of hawsers and fenders – the oddest English she had ever heard.

'Where do they come from?' she gestured at the wharf. The captain's wife had visited many ports.

'Some of them will be Kanakas from the Pacific Islands I expect – they jump ship often enough. Some of them will be natives, of course. And then there are always those roustabouts – Italians, Portuguese, Irish – you know what the Irish are like, my dear – who have drifted around the world to end up at this unlikely spot. Adventurers they call themselves.'

and was she not one also?

no, we don't know how she came. we know only that she was appointed teacher for the second term of the mill school's first year. a widow, they said (a safe bet), she would have been educated, she would have spoken a proper English, the Queen's they said. after all this was *British* Columbia, 1873.

The day was frosty still in places where the sun, blocked by buildings, by the massive bulk of trees, of mountains even, had failed to penetrate. A subtle white sparkle, ethereal as powder. And everything else legible, easily read: the rawness of new wood, the brashness of cleared land, of hastily built houses, outhouses, leantos. And beyond them, the endless green of woods, a green so green it outgreened itself, hill after hill. When she turned she could see the mountains behind her hanging close, close and yet aloof. Beautiful, she thought, or perilous. But not pretty. Well-versed in the Romantics, she had arrived with images of the Alps inside her eyes. Yet she knew this was not Europe and Mary Shelley's monster would never speak his loneliness here.

––––––––

i learned to stay in the house as a good girl should. i am still in the house i move around in all day in the rain, the kids in school, Richard at it, at school as he calls the campus, reducing it to the scale of Mickey's elementary, why? they all do it, all the faculty, as if belittling, and maybe it is, the forced rote of teaching the same course year after year. when i go there i see library, see centuries of hidden knowledge, wealth, see romance – like you in this, Ina, how you used to enter the North Van library as if entering a medieval cloister, sssh, you warned, as if trespassing, pulling me into the smell of dust, of breath bated between plastic covers, heading immediately for the shelf of historical novels, family history with its lurid stretches shaping the destiny of a nation. consoled by this, that the familial, the mundane, could actually have historic proportions? kings and queens in bed with you of an afternoon. rain, rain.

you might as well learn some history, you said, handing me *The Old Curiosity Shoppe* (both volumes), *The Scarlet Pimpernel*, drawing distinctions between trash and literature. you might as well learn, you said, and blamed me later for becoming a 'blue-stocking – I can't even *talk* to you,' when i got my degree (BA only, mind you, ending my graduate career by getting pregnant and marrying Richard). 'i'm marrying my history prof,' i

16

said, hoping to shock you. but you were pleased. trained to exhibit a 'good mind,' but only 'within reason' – reason being utilitarian, education as part of 'attractiveness' leading to marriage – i ended up doing what i was meant to, i followed the plotline through, the story you had me enact.

and now you're dead, Ina, the story has abandoned me. i can't seem to stay on track, nor can my sentence, even close its brackets. you didn't teach me about asides, you never told me the 'right track' is full of holes, pot-holes of absence (sleeping pills and social smiles, 'i'm fine, fine,' hanging on.) i don't even want to 'pull yourself together,' as Richard urges (myself? yourself? theirself), 'after all, grieving can't bring her back, you've got your own life to lead, you've got us.' true. (that reasonable word again.) but something isn't.

i've been moving around the house all day in the rain, in the growing dark outside, far from leading my own life or my life leading anywhere (goodbye, hero), i feel myself in you, irritated at the edges where we overlap. it occurs to me you died of reason (thunder far off on the edges of town and always i think it's missiles going off): i mean explanation, justification, normal mental state – that old standard.

the dictionary, your immigrant weapon, Ina, saves me when the words stop, when the names stick ... real? you said, what is 'real cute'? Canadians don't know how to speak proper English. real is an adjective, look, and you showed me in the dictionary: true, actual. true cute? it doesn't make sense. you can say it's either true or cute, but not both. too true.

was dying a way of stopping all those words, all those variable terms, true or not? because it's hopeless ('hopeless,' you said, 'you'll never learn'), this task of trying to muffle them to one. true: exactly conforming to a rule, standard, or pattern; trying to sing true. by whose standard or rule? and what do you do when the true you feel inside sounds different from the standard?

i want to talk to you. (now? now when it's too late?) i want to say something. tell you something about the bush and what you were afraid of, what i escaped to: anonymous territory where names faded to a tiny hubbub, lost in all that other noise – the soughing, sighing of bodies, the cracks and chirps, odd rustles, something like breath escaping, something inhuman i slipped through. in communion with trees, following the migratory routes of bugs, the pathways of water, the warning sounds of birds, i was native, i was the child who grew up with wolves, original lost girl, elusive, vanished from the world of men ...

but you, a woman, walked with the possibility of being seen, ambushed in the sudden arms of bears or men. 'never go into the woods with a man,' you said, 'and don't go into the woods alone.'

we knew about bears. sometimes they would raid our garbage cans at night and the phones would ring all up and down the block, there's a bear at the Potts', keep the dogs and kids inside. excitement, peering through the windows out at street-light pooling gravel. so they were real then? shambling shadows, garbage-eaters, only a little larger than the Newfoundland next door. but with something canny in them, resistant to attempts to scare them off, looking over their shoulders with contempt, four-footed men in shaggy suits intent on a meal.

'if a man talks to you on the street, don't answer him,' you said.

'but what if he wants directions? what if he wants a dime?' we asked. 'just keep walking,' you said. but we saw you fish for quarters when the men shambled up to you on the street outside department stores, we watched you in your trim black coat, well-tailored, your little hat, we watched you scrambling around in your purse for change, and it was true, you didn't say a word, though you did respond, awkward and flushed. when we asked if that's what you meant, you said it wasn't that.

skid row was a name we learned. rape was a word that was hidden from us. 'but what would he do?' 'bad things you wouldn't like.'

our bodies were ours as far as we knew and we knew what we liked, laughing exhausted and sweaty in our fort or wiping bloody knees with leaves and creek water. without history we squatted in needle droppings to pee, flung our bodies through the trees – we would have swung on vines if there had been any, as it was we swung on vine maples. always we imagined we were the first ones there, the first trespassers –

*if you go down in the woods today you'd better go in disguise.* it was bears' territory we entered, or cedars'. it was the land of skunk cabbage. it was not ours and no one human, no man preceded us.

*'The red cedar, unequalled as a wood for shingles, comes next to the fir in importance. Because of its variety of shading, and the brilliant polish which it takes, it is prized for the interior finishing of houses. As the cedar lasts well underground it is used for telegraph poles and*

*fence posts ... Well can this wood be called the settler's friend, for from it he can with simple tools, such as axe and saw, build his house, fence his farm, and make his furniture.'*

without history or use, sitting in the middle of the rain forest, an immigrant school teacher wrote: 'To touch the soft finger-lings of Fir, the scaly fronds of Cedar! – Underfoot, a veritable pelt of needle droppings. If Earth be sentient here, then Man with his machinery, his noisy saw, his clanking chain and bit, is afterall dwarf in such green fur, mere Insect only. – It comforts me.'

well-read. she must have been. writing with a touch of the sub-lime, that nineteenth-century sense of grandeur, in her immaculate teacher's handwriting.

you would never write like that. not just because of your blunt sprawled hand, so impossible to read, huge words that took up all the space on the scraps of paper you left: '2 homo pls.' '2 brown,' but because of the grade-school scribbler you hid under your bed and which you showed me once, family stories for *The Reader's Digest,* 'Laughter is the Best Medicine,' stories that lost their humour in description, faded away in proper sentences. 'tell me the truth: they're terrible, aren't they?' you who could outtalk, outname, outargue me anytime.

Mrs. Richards wrote for herself, her English self she wanted to lose in the trees, trees we have already lost. trees so big men lay inside the gash their axes left and the tree still standing, still

20

*trees*

joined to part of itself. so big men balanced on boards wedged
in the trunk to cut it down, or had pictures made of themselves
standing victorious on top of the fallen length, oxen waiting to
haul it away.

and though we didn't know it then in the 1950s when we came,
we saw only second growth, the mountain logged off long ago
to feed Moody's mill, or Stamp's (no, where we were was
Moody's territory – they were jealous of their territory, those
lumber-barons). we didn't know that then, penetrating undergrowth thick with fern and salal (itself a sign), salmonberry,
thimbleberry, all the berry bushes obscuring trails long over-
grown.

we couldn't have imagined the world Mrs. Richards walked
into, a man's world of work, of mud the odd boardwalk
covered. a world of leantos and lanterns, of sudden accident, of
jokes and brawls to punctuate long hours of labour. by 1873
she is there, named in the pages of history as 'Mrs. Richards, a
young and pretty widow' who fills the suddenly vacated post of
school teacher.

when she arrived she walked into sawdust, a sprawling con-
glomeration of sheds alive with dogs, pigs, chickens. 'what is
the meaning of this agglomeration of filth?' Captain Raymur
had thundered through his Protestant Halifax whiskers in
1869. in 1873, though it still shuts down for several days when
there's a gambling game and though Raymur hasn't been able
to stop the traffic down the two-plank walk to Granville saloons
– 'a lovely walk on a hot day' – the mill boasts a brand new
school, a post office in its store, a few front parlours, several
ladies now in residence. ('ladies'?) listen, there is even the

21

sound of a piano tinkling through the smoke of clearing fires.
someone is playing Chopin ...

— now you're exaggerating.

— how would you know?

— you always did. you should've gone into theatre, not history.

— i mean how would you know what this place was like? you
never read about it, you were never interested in any past
outside of England's.

— well think about it. who would play Chopin in a grimy
little milltown? who would even appreciate it? no one
appreciates good music here, they think it's snobbish,
what do they call it? uppercrust. and this is supposed to be
a city!

— there you go, always criticizing this place for its lack of
culture. as if we were living somewhere out in the bush.

— we may as well be, and it's only provincialism that stops
you from seeing it. we should've packed you off to boarding school in England long ago. then you'd know something about culture.

the smoky glass swan drifting in a pool of tears. les sylphides.
the forlorn Soho flowergirl haunting the blue wall of the room i
practised and practised in. music meant the moonlight sonata,
meant someplace else, not history (i thought vaguely of the
plaster busts lined up on Mrs. Pritchett's grand piano —

Beethoven looking burgherish, Mozart looking slightly mad, they meant nothing to me), it wasn't the music i escaped to but the aura of tears, of blue walls, of infinite lemon layers of furniture polish. polish, everything said, in the grace is the promise. (that lie you spent hours perfecting.) i breathed it like incense after the hot betrayals of locker rooms, the ridicule of notes, of whispered gossip. my difference i was trying to erase. my English shoes and woolly vests. my very words.

impasse: 'my very words' were yours. ✳ *whose?*

woollies and sweeties, hotties and hermits for tea, honeybunch. all the comforts of home when the world of school, the public world (not private – that was another confusion), the schoolyard world of who likes / who cuts who, got to be too much. Miss Goody-Two-Shoes, stuck-up. i knew those words too. just as i knew gah-gah and common. sweater's such a common word, darling, can't you say woolly, say cardigan? say, who do you think you are? (yes, who? who?) you think you're really something, don't you? but you're weird (different, foreign), eating that stuff! (curry tarts in my lunchbox) looks like puke! i'd vomit too if i had to eat hot dogs. Hot Dog, the creep talks! and niggerbabies and chickenbones. that's just candy. it's sweets, boiled or not. it's what you buy with pocket money. at least we had pennies in common. but who else said, do you want to spend a penny? meaning, go to the washroom. i mean the lavatory, i mean the loo. the ladies, let's say. at least you asked for the ladies as we stood embarrassed by you in department stores. two languages. two allegiances.

impasse: impossible to exit. dead end. when the walls close down. the public / private wall. defined the world you lived inside, the world you brought with you, transposed, onto a

*women?*

23

Salish mountainside. and never questioned its terms. 'lady.'
never questioned its values. English gentility in a rain forest?

o the cultural labyrinth of our inheritance, mother to daughter
to mother ...

– and i suppose you see me as the monster hidden at the
heart of it?

there *is* a monster, there is something monstrous here, but it's
not you. i saw you as something else when i was running down
the road late for school. i could hear the bell ringing, the sound
of thundering feet, the jostling, giggling. could smell tomato-
rice soup already reeking from the closed kitchen, mixed with
the smell of sweat, of pencil shavings, hear the clock ticking in
the Principal's Office. late again. the sound of the word
DETENTION, pink slip like a flag in my hands as i opened the
door and all those faces slowly turned to eye me, ascertain my
fear in the pause before Miss Skalder's words would send me
to my seat. the road so quiet, long, my feet so slow, i wondered
what you did in the empty house alone, one in a row of houses
settled in the sunlight, dreaming. all the housewives absent,
their curlerheads, their still mops on their knees in the after-
math of storm. endless morning stretched before them, ten-
drils of quiet crept in their windows, hours of nothing slipped
through their doors. bathrobe sleeping beauties gone in a trice,
a trance, embalmed, waiting for a kiss to wake them when their
kids, their men would finally come home. how peaceful i
thought, how i longed for it, a woman's place. safe. suspended
out of the swift race of the world.

the monstrous lie of it: the lure of absence. self-effacing.

24

*'Watch Carter when the "donk" (his donkey!) has got up steam – its first steam; and when the rigging men (his rigging men!) drag out the wire rope to make a great circle through the woods. And when the circle is complete from one drum, round by where the cut logs are lying, back to the other drum; and when the active rigging slinger (his rigging slinger!) has hooked a log on to a point of the wire cable; and when the signaller (his signaller!) has pulled the wire telegraph and made the donkey toot ... just think of Carter's feelings as the engineer jams over levers, opens up the throttle, sets the thudding, whirring donkey winding up the cable, and drags the first log into sight; out from the forest down to the beach; bump, bump! Think what this mastery over huge, heavy logs means to a man who has been used to coax them to tiny movements by patience and a puny jack-screw ...'*

history the story, Carter's and all the others', of dominance. mastery. the bold line of it.

soon it will be getting dark, soon the kids will be coming in from outdoors, Mickey breathless and exuberant from hockey practise, Ange drifting in the door with studied boredom and the latest 'grunge' about school. and what will i have done with my day, this endless day that unites and separates us? it is the kind of waiting you knew.

moving around in a maze of things to be done, the little ones that never get finished because there is always more i should, i could be doing ... the rotting walls of resolution, good intention, will power.

how you repainted them. Bapco apple green, primrose yellow. painting them over and over. Kem-Tone blue. blue willow covering up the cracks, the tears in the wallpaper. faultlines. faults. so fix your hair, mend your ways. to fix up a home is fixing up yourself. Practice Makes Perfect, over and over. the smell of turps in the rusty red Blue Ribbon can, later the latex and rollers. you loved it, we said, not knowing. 'love.' the constant reek of it, the glazed feel on your skin, transformation via aching arm, something achieved at last: long hours of the mind alone in its trap turning the wheel.

Ina, i remember you with flecks of paint, hair wisps escaping from under your peasant scarf (it's a kerchief, we said – we wore them to school with the others practising femininity). i work like a peasant, you said. your peasant scarf then, that made you look severe except for the soft line of your cheek, paint sprottled on its down. always the frownlines etched deeper between your eyes, etched by trying, arm in the air for hours, to paint a ceiling, paint a face, paint over the cracks in the whole setup.

holes. there were holes in the story you had inherited. holes in the image. Canada: romance of the wilds, to which you brought:

a trunkful of woolly underwear. Mounties in red coats and Rose-Marie. the loons, the lost lakes. a pas-de-deux, glittering, white, under the lights of theatre marquees and furs ...

26

not knowing there was first of all:

*'a clearing three hundred and fifty yards along the shore, two hundred and fifty yards into the forest, boxed in by tall trees; damp, wet, the actual clearing littered with stumps and forest debris, and a profusion of undergrowth, including luxuriant skunk cabbage.'*

not knowing there was first of all a mill and then:

*'three hotels: Deighton's, Sunnyside, and Joe Mannion's; one grocery store, and Chinese wash house, and lock-up.'*

to elaborate:

beer parlours separated into men's and ladies-and-escorts. movie houses and oyster bars. the everpresent five-and-dime. skid row churches and drunks and countless patrol cars careening, sirens wailing, traffic flickering in the growing night.

and that was 1950, that was what we came into, Ina, stepping off the train into mythic snow one dark November afternoon. and Harald was there and the bridge was there and all those flickering lights, a necklace looping us into the North Shore of our future.

 – the trouble with you, Annie, is that you want to tell a story,
    no matter how much history you keep throwing at me.

 – and i know what that means, you who used to accuse me
    of 'telling stories' when you thought i'd lied.

27

– you've forgotten how many stories i used to tell you when you were small.

– but then you stopped telling them, or told me to stop telling them – 'telling stories again?'

– it was you who changed. you grew up. you learned the difference between story and history.

i learned that history is the real story the city fathers tell of the only important events in the world. a tale of their exploits hacked out against a silent backdrop of trees, of wooden masses. so many claims to fame. so many ordinary men turned into heroes. (where are the city mothers?) the city fathers busy building a town out of so many shacks labelled the Western Terminus of the Transcontinental, Gateway to the East – all these capital letters to convince themselves of its, of their, significance.

*'A world event had happened in Vancouver ... On the eve of the Queen's Birthday, 1887, the Canadian Pacific Railway ... closed the last gap in the "All-Red Route," and raised the obscure settlement on the muddy shore of Water Street, sobriquetly termed "Gastown," to the status of a world port.'* Major Matthews.

all the figures, facts to testify to their being present at it:

*'I had 400 men working 140 in a tented camp one third mile west of the hotel. I built the two and one half miles of the* CPR *from Hastings to Hastings Sawmill ...'* John ('Chinese') McDougall.

*'I hauled logs with oxen down Gore Avenue, also out of the Park at*

*Brockton Point, had a logging camp at Greer's Beach (Kitsilano),
and another on Granville Street at False Creek.'* H.S. Rowlings.

I / my laying track with facts rescued against the obscurity of
bush. and the women moving about their rooms all day in the
rain, remembering:

*'The first piano on the south side of Burrard Inlet was one which was
part of the cabin furniture of the barque "Whittier," Captain and
Mrs. Schwappe. Mrs. Schwappe sold it to Mrs. Richards, school
teacher, who lived in a little three-room cottage back of the Hastings
Mill Schoolhouse ...'* Alice Patterson.

what is a 'world event'? getting a piano was a world event in that
'obscure settlement' because years later somebody still
remembered it, even remembered where it came from and
who bought it. Mrs. Schwappe. Mrs. Richards. a ship's piano
suddenly landed in an out-of-the-way spot, this little three-
room cottage. these are not facts but skeletal bones of a
suppressed body the story is. <u>there *is* a story here,</u> Ina, i keep
trying to get to. it begins:

... At the other end of a square of light cast on the dark outside,
unknown trees, sawdust and stump debris, a woman was sitting
at an oilcloth-covered table, blue and white check (no, that was
the picnic cloth you used to use – did they have oilcloth in
1873?). perhaps she brought a lace one with her when she
came over, one of her mother's (we know nothing about her
mother). she was sitting in the pool of light, yellow and rather
dim to our eyes, the coal oil lantern cast. sitting and writing in
that journal of hers that later, years later would be stored in the
dustfree atmosphere of city archives. she was writing what

29

would become a record, but then, then her hand hovered, her mind jumped, she could have imagined anything and written it down as real forever — *history*

'Such rain here! – It rains day in and day out, a veritable curtain falling all around my Cabin. The trees weep, paths slip into small bogs, the chickens look as bedraggled as I feel my muddy skirts to be. I am orphaned here at the end of the world – Yet I feel no grief, for I am made new here, Father, solitary as I am – nor am I entirely so: daily a garrulous blue-black bird keeps me company, the young Cedar spared by my front door dips to greet me. Nor do these tell me what I must be.'

she writes as if she were living alone in the woods, her vision trued to trees and birds. she filters out the hive of human activity in which her 'cabin' sits, a tiny cell of light, late, after the others have been extinguished. in the dark (i imagine her writing at night, on the other side of a day in England she already knew) she can overlook the stumps, the scarred face of the clearing that surrounds her, and see herself ab-original in the new world (it is the old one she is at the end of). but why she had to erase so much is never given. it is part of what is missing, like her first name, like her past that has dropped away. we cannot see her and so she is free to look out at the world with her own eyes, free to create her vision of it. this is not history.

and this is why, perhaps, they think her journal suspect at the archives. 'inauthentic,' fictional possibly, contrived later by a daughter who imagined (how ahistoric) her way into the unspoken world of her mother's girlhood. girl? even then, teaching at Hastings Mill, she was said to be a widow, though young. but she married again, didn't she? she married Ben Springer and moved across the inlet to Moodyville, Moody's mill, the rival one. and her daughter? we know nothing of her, this possible interpreter of her mother's place in that world. it's hardly a record of that world, is it? no, it's Mrs. Richards' private world, at least that's what they call it. that's why it's not historical – a document, yes, but not history. you mean it's not factual.

what is fact? (f) act. the f stop of act. a still photo in the ongoing cinerama.

Mrs. Patterson, say, with her crocheted mitts and bonnet, the very picture of a 'Dame Hospitaller.' there is no image of Mrs. Richards. but if there were, she would be caught with a tiny frown between her eyes, lower lip dented by an apprehensive finger, pen idle before her, thinking:

'My keenest pleasure is to walk the woods, despite their scolding me most roundly as to its dangers. I do not hold stock in their stories of Bears! – The Siwash do not seem to fear them but wander as they will. If need be, I will lie face down as if dead, as they have told me.'

'More I fear their talk about me, their Suppositions. Perhaps because they understand me to be a Widow, the men think me most eager for their company. Capt. Soule yesterday insisted on escorting me, pointing out this and that – D'ye see those two peaks beyond the Inlet? he says, Sheba's Paps they call 'em. I did not know whether to shew myself insulted, for surely a School Mistress should be above reproach. Yet it was laughable – what did he imagine Sheba to be? I merely remarked that Burrard's Inlet must look very different from the Nile, which gave him the occasion to boast, Indeed ye'd get no timbers the size of ours from that desert. And so it passed. Should I have shown displeasure at a remark a gentleman would not utter in the company of a lady? And he a member of the School Board! Or does he speak freely because he sees me wandering of my own free will? I cannot keep only to drawing rooms and the School! I am not a Proper Lady perhaps.'

Proper, she says, Lady capitalized, and it is barely sounded, the relationship between proper and property. the other Ladies at the mill would be wives or daughters-about-to-be-wives: Mrs. Alexander, Mrs. Patterson, Miss Sweney. she alone is without 'protection,' as they would say. subject, then, to sly advances under the guise of moral detection, subject to agonzing (your word, Ina), subject to self-doubt in a situation without clearly defined territory (because she is no one's property, she is 'free' without being sexually free), she feels her difference from the other women, hopes the Captain recognizes it as freedom of intellect (suspects he doesn't), is at home only with things without language (birds, trees) in a place she struggles to account for in her own words. words, that shifting territory. never one's own. full of deadfalls and hidden claims to a reality others have made.

lady, for instance. a word that has claimed so much from women trying to maintain it. the well-ironed linen, clean (lace at the cuffs, at the collar), well-tailored dresses and wraps, the antimacassars, lace tablecloths, the christening bonnets. beyond that, a certain way of walking, of talking. and always that deference, that pleased attention to the men who gave them value, a station in life, a reason for existing. lady, *hlaēfdige,* kneader of bread, mistress of a household, lady of the manor, woman of good family, woman of refinement and gentle manners, a woman whose conduct conforms to a certain standard of propriety ('lady airs' – singing true again).

i imagine the ladies of Hastings Mill spent hours when they got together discussing the merits of various haberdashers in Victoria, New Westminster, centres of culture by comparison with Granville and the mill store with its red flannel. so hard to get anything 'decent,' they complained. for a decent lady kept herself well-covered, her sexuality hidden. no flag to taunt 'vigorous' men with. for if men couldn't control their desires, women could. women knew the standard of what was socially acceptable in conduct and apparel. just as you spent hours, Ina, shopping for bargains, shopping department store basements or poring over Sears catalogues, dismissing things that looked 'cheap,' vainly trying to clothe us with the class you had in the tropics where your clothes were handsewn by Chinese tailors and our intricately smocked dresses came from the School for the Blind. now there was very little money and Harald wore good suits that 'lasted' ('slightly out of date, poor dear'), you tried bargain dresses ('dreadful – people here have no idea of fashion'), and struggled with our running around in jeans – 'so unladylike.' exactly. skirts meant keeping your legs together as you so often told me (i didn't realize *why*), skirts meant girdles and garter belts and stockings ...

– and i suppose it wasn't *your* crinolines i had to starch?

– i remember. crinolines and white bucks.

– and i suppose it wasn't you who pestered me for high heels?

– but it wasn't that i wanted to be a 'lady,' i wanted to be like the other girls, sexy but not too much, just enough to be liked, just enough to be cute.

– and what about 'nice'?

33

yes, nice girls don't ... i didn't realize the only alternative to lady you knew, was tramp, though that was a line i heard often enough on one of your records. tramps were girls who smoked in the bushes behind the corner store (doo-wop, doo-wop). tramps loved Chuck Berry and *Little Darlin'*, wore pencil-line skirts with kick pleats, wobbled their hips, inked initials on their arms. tramps cut school or left it because they had to. i was fascinated with their flouting all the rules, but i didn't want to be one. tramp was a word nice girls used to brand those outside their group – tramp, slut, bitch. *— hierarchy w/i gender*

i came home to *Red Roses for a Blue Lady*, the last pop song you bought. i came home to the peculiar silence of your growing naps, your obsessive washing the kitchen floor, your chronic exhaustion (sleep, the one great unsatisfied desire). 'that damn dog, they deliberately leave it out all night to torture me.' 'hell's bells, will no one give me any peace?' peace. a lady's respect for tranquility.

> *Oh, Jemima, look at your Uncle Jim,*
> *He's in the duck pond, learning how to swim;*
> *First he does the breast stroke, then he does the side,*
> *And now he's under the water, swimming against the*
> *tide.*

i didn't hear then what kind of stroking was meant. bathing was what you called swimming, as if to sanitize it. what did you do with all that pent-up energy? (besides paint walls) you taught us your fear, you taught us what you knew about a world where even uncles were not to be trusted. you grew more afraid as our sexuality came budding to the fore – foreground, fore-body, carrying these forward parts of our bodies. ladies do not draw attention to themselves. (is that you speaking or your mother or

34

all the mothers?) ladies keep to the background. ladies *are* the soothing background their men come home to.

'The man suggests that he would like chicken for dinner. It is not a command, yet such is the harmony between them that his wishes are hers,' says one of your how-to-heal / how-to-fix yourself books (caught in a fix, castrated – what is the female word for it? i mean for the psychological condition?) Soul has 'positively no wishes of its own, no preferences. It stands for-ever as the servant of Spirit' and in this it is 'similar to a happy home.' the standard. Soul: generic feminine. it is the man who is Spirit, has spirit. what does Soul, what does a woman do with her unexpressed preferences, her own desires? (damned up, a torrent to let loose.) and this is what you were trying to live up to. the neuter.

a book of interruptions is not a novel


what is her first name? she must have one –
so far she has only the name of a dead man,
someone somewhere else

No one knows when she came or how long she had been there when she was appointed school teacher. Or even whose widow she was. She arrives in the records in the fall of 1873.

*'Miss Sweney was shortly succeeded by Mrs. Richards, who soon became Mrs. Ben Springer and cast her lot with the struggling little hamlet, giving place to a Miss Redfern ... great difficulty was experienced in keeping a teacher longer than six months.'*

Richards, unlisted, should follow Reid, Mrs., who arrived in 1884, was saved with her children in the Great Fire of '86 by crouching in a ditch under blankets kept constantly wet by D.R. Reid, whose 'hat and coat were burned off him.'

Richards should precede Rickets, E.R., bank manager responsible for ensuring that Vancouver was given 'a day on the official programme' of the Royal Tour of 1901.

in actual fact, Ana Richards, precedes both and fades into the northern shoreline of Burrard Inlet as Mrs. Springer of Moodyville, of whom we hear nothing more.

\*

*'The present is decidedly an age of civilization. One of the chief signs of progress in this respect is the possessing a local paper. Moodyville, then, can now claim to be, what it really is, a go-ahead, prosperous, civilized locality. For here is the proof – here is its newspaper!'*

\*

Stepping out, locking the door behind her, locking herself out of the now familiar smell of grubby clothes and chalk, she felt emptied at last into the open air. Let sunshine take her, that time of day when siding, rooftops, glowed in the smoky distance. Turning the corner, she could see the long low roof of the mill and the plume from its waste fire burning against blue mountains – curious how the mountains approached or receded depending on the air. Today they seemed far away, erased by everything shining in between. Even the piles of freshcut lumber seemed to invite her eye to run along their surface – it *was* a kind of stripping, the tree stripped down to its bare flesh. And everything thick, a kind of hair in the world, even the earth her boots sank into, powder earth composed of rootlets and fir mulch, a fibrous mass. She could walk forever on an afternoon like this – let down her hair, feel her skin expand beyond the confines of her clothes. She wanted to kick off her boots, dance the well-being of her soul at home, for once, in her skin.

If only she could write it down, as if the words might make a place she could re-enter when she felt the need, when she forgot – what it was like to feel this complete.

\*

'... *drawing scanty draughts of inspiration from nought but the plaintive melody of a couple of Thomas Cats, who nightly haunt the*

40

*classic precincts of "Brigham Terrace." Under these slightly adverse circumstances it is that the Editor craves your forbearance.'*

\*

She checked through her basket – the recitation book from which she must choose a passage, the test papers which must be marked – and, yes, she had her diary with her. She would walk to her spot in the woods where she could write in the midst of all this plenty undisturbed. Except by birds, the rustling of wings, an occasional snap that made her lift her head. Still, if she wrote outdoors the words might gather on the page with this thick being she could feel between things, undisturbed.

And then she felt rather than heard the tread, turned. Two Siwash in white men's clothes. Looking gloomy, dark even. Possibly come from the mill where they had asked for work and not received it. But the short one, hair fallen over his face, looked consumptive, too weak for that. Perhaps they had taken fish to the cookhouse – but then they would be heading towards the beach where their dugout lay. What should she say? She turned and continued walking, felt them gaining on her. Turned again. The tall one swayed a little. Were they drunk? 'They go crazy when they drink,' she heard Mrs. Patterson say, 'we can't stop the shiphands from trading them liquor.' They did not look drunk. Advanced rather, with a steady tread, a sombre determination. Perhaps they were furious and meant to do her harm. She should say Good day, something civil, but she froze on the path as they approached, sick with the stories she had heard: Stackeye axing Perry in his sleep, Mrs. Sullivan menaced with a knife. It was the sickness of fear and they knew it as they crowded past her as if she were a bush, a fern shaking in their way.

\*

*'Interesting and so-called "live" information from "Special Correspondents" at the Logging Camps as to the prevalence of mosquitoes or other wise, the state of the roads (if any), probable changes in the weather, stale, rehashed articles on the Eastern Question and Chinese Emigration, with estimates of the computed strength of "Fell's Coffee" over Chicory — all these items shall be dwelt upon in the length common to the other local journals of this Province, thereby enabling us to accomplish the feat of rendering the "TICKLER" as unreadable as most of its contemporaries!'*

\*

A huckleberry bush, red with the same red that suffused her face. She was ashamed, no, she was furious at herself as she stood there and watched their receding backs. They were walking away slowly and only themselves, amused, she thought, with a kind of silent laughter. They had merely passed a white woman in the woods while she, she was sure to be killed. And now there was nothing left of the day but this foolishness quivering through her legs, her head gone wooden again.

you misspelled her name

*Ana*

that's her name:
   back, backward, reversed
   again, anew

she was knocking on paper, not wood, tapping like someone blind along the wall of her solitude. under the white light of concentration, the paper yielded nothing but white noise – a whispering of trees outside in the wind, the low buzz of anxiety – ill-lit streets and bears or men, Ange (only fifteen, and not a baby she reminded herself) wandering out there with friends. the sound of Mickey's radio in his room, Richard's typewriter busy upstairs were comforts of some kind, ongoing. the kind of noise that could occupy her mind, if she would let it.

but there was the page, her tapping there, looking for a way out of the blank that faced her – blankety-blank – and not that tug either, the elliptical tug of memory which erased this other. she was looking for the company of another who was also reading – out through the words, through the wall that separated her, an arm, a hand –

and so she began, 'a woman sitting at her kitchen table writing,' as if her hand holding the pen could embody the very feel of a life. as if she could reach out and touch her, those lashes cast down over blue (brown?) eyes, the long line of nose, the lips doubting or pleased, that curve of a shoulder, upper arm, wrist at another table in a different kind of light (no street lights there, no advertising crawling the sky. the stars she saw whenever she went out to pee must have patterned the dark with increasing layers of brilliance, starlight coming in, ancient and unreadable news ...) no, it's this small and present thing her arm, her hand holding the pen between which fingers of which hand: lefthanded and upright, or right and oblique in the proper fashion? dipping into the ink, scratching fine hesitancies on the too-soft paper of a school scribbler ... does she stare at the wall? as if the right, the only word might suddenly appear? not brown, or not merely brown (it isn't starlight she's seeing, fingers over her eyes, thumb on one cheekbone the better to think), but darker than tea ...

'I try again – It seems no foot, or none other than mine, disturbs the living intimacy of these Ferns and small Bushes, the roots of enormous Trees going down into – its brackish waters evade the eye – 'Tis a nameless colour as if stained by the Trees themselves, darker than tea ...'

what is she editing out and for whom? besides herself? it is herself there though she writes 'the' eye and not 'my.' objective: out there and real (possibly) to others. she is thinking about those possible others leaning over her shoulder as she writes. or does she strive only to capture in words a real she feels beyond her? those enormous Trees with their capital letter. a colour no word can convey. i lean over her shoulder as she tries, as she doubts: why write at all? why not leave the place as wordless as she finds it? because there is 'into –' what? frightening preposition. into the unspoken urge of a body insisting itself in the words.

who's there? (knock, knock). who else is there in this disappearing act when you keep leaving yourself behind the next bend. given that 'yourself' is everything you've been, the trail leading backwards and away from you behind your feet. evident. named. recognizable in fact. it isn't Frankenstein you're looking for but some elusive sense of who you might be: she, unspoken and real in the world, running ahead to embrace it.

46

she is writing her desire to be, in the present tense, retrieved from silence. each morning she begins with all their names. she has taught them to say, 'Present, Mrs. Richards,' and so, each morning she begins with her name, a name that is not really hers. each evening she enters her being, nameless, in the book she is writing against her absence. for nothing that surrounds her is absent. far from it.

there are photographs of the buildings, of the docks, of the men. there are maps of the streets, the first few blocks of Granville or Gastown (Gassy Jack's town, the appropriative hidden in the abbreviation). there are histories of properties changing hands and names, of civic developments named for those who pushed them through. amidst all this there are brief references to women: Mrs. John Peabody Patterson, practical nurse and wife of the loading supervisor at Hastings Mill, 'the sort of hardboiled angel of mercy Gastown needed,' Alan Morley sketches her. or Mrs. Richard Henry Alexander, wife of the assistant manager and 'social queen of the inlet' (Morley again), a Scots girl who came over on one of the brideships to marry a man and a station. there are two women entrepreneurs in Gastown, 'devout Mrs. Sullivan, a mulatto (who) set up a tiny restaurant,' and Birdie Stewart, 'Vancouver's first madam,' whose arrival coincides with that of Mrs. Richards. there is even a photographic portrait of Mrs. Patterson, giving her full name, Emily Susan née Branscombe, the only full name of a woman given. her face still bearing the soft contours of youth (she is perhaps twenty-eight), mitted hands clasped properly at her waist, broad lace collar, dark hair looped gracefully under the black bow-cap, she looks out at us with a slightly bemused and level gaze, every inch a lady and scarcely 'hardboiled.'

but only the briefest mention is made of Mrs. Richards who takes over the job of schoolteacher when her predecessor, Georgia or Julia Sweeney or Sweney, 'daughter of the mill-wright,' having lasted one term leaves to get married. Morley, on what grounds (a stroke of journalistic logic? romantic deduction?) describes Mrs. Richards as a 'young and pretty widow,' perhaps from the following entry in Matthews:

*'The first piano on the south side of Burrard Inlet was one which was ... sold to Mrs. Richards, school teacher, who lived in a little three-room cottage back of the Hastings Mill schoolhouse, and afterwards married Ben Springer.'*

the sweep of that part of her life summed up: she buys a piano and afterwards marries Ben Springer, as if they were cause and effect, these acts. history is the historic voice (voice-over), elegiac, epithetic. a diminishing glance as the lid is closed firmly and finally shut. that was her. summed up. Ana historic.

and it is Alice Patterson who remembers and tells Matthews. Alice, one of Susan Patterson's daughters who composed four of the fifteen pupils necessary to start a government-funded school. in that brief statement there is nothing of the friendship that existed between these women a generation older than Alice. nothing of the unspoken sharing of their lives. something is lacking. in 1874 Mrs. Richards marries Ben Springer and the Pattersons move to Moodyville. that is all that history says.

but i don't want history's voice. i want ... something is wanting in me. and it all goes blank on a word. want. what does it mean, to be lacking? empty. wanton. vanish. vacant, vacuum, evacuate. all these empty words except for wanton (lacking disci-

48

pline, lewd). a word for the wild. for the gap i keep coming to. i keep pointing out to you, Ina, as if it could somehow have stopped your dying. your going. gone. your one wanton act ('rebellious,' even that is obsolete). as Richard's mother said: 'she must have just got tired of trying.'

i am trying very hard to speak, to tell it. why you didn't or couldn't. i have passed through the guilt, that it was all my fault, if only i'd seen more of you, found the right question, argued more, provoked you into a torrent of speech, the torrent you dammed up all those later years – after they had fixed you, patched you up. the torrent you used to release in rushes of fury on our innocent heads. (we thought we were innocent and perhaps we were because we couldn't understand our part in it, we the children and so by definition innocent.)

– if you, or i, can believe it.

– and what is that supposed to mean?

– you know very well. you were never innocent, you, the oldest. always harping on this or that – all the ways i failed to 'understand' you.

– that's what Ange claims, i suppose all daughters do. but i tried so hard to be 'good.' Dad said i held us all together.

– yes, you were the Perfect Little Mother, weren't you? you could have replaced me. you tried hard enough.

trying. a trying child. trying it on for size. the role. all that she had been told would make her a woman. (knock, knock.) would she ever be one?

she was walking down the back steps, self-consciously, slowly. it wasn't where she was going but what she was walking, her body, out into the world. not wanting to get anywhere fast (not that headlong rush, two steps at a time, that simple intent where she was one with the going which she identified now as childish.) now she was walking her body as if it were different from her, her body with its new look. (o the luck, to be looked at. o the lack, if you weren't. o the look. looking as if it all depended on it.) peach, she looks a peach in her sweater with its collar at the open and curving neck her neck curves up from, above, now, two mounds, small, but two (too?) peach-coloured lobes (she would almost hide) held, up to the world in her new bra like two hands relentlessly cupping her breasts to view. and her whole body is different now, walks slowly with a certain held-in (she is held, by elastic) grace, hand trailing down the familiar rail of the back steps she no longer wants to jump, her feet turn at the bottom and head slowly toward the carport, to the rockery beyond. she knows where he is, gardening on Saturday as usual in his baggy garden khakis, old hat on to keep the sun off his sensitive face. she will think of something to say (it's lunchtime, Dad), she will stand there self-consciously waiting, idle, smelling the earth his hands turn over as they uproot the last of the autumn dahlias, waiting until he turns to look at her with that quizzical smile, accepting in its affection (hand ruffling her hair when she was younger) – and I suppose you've only just had breakfast, Princess? and she will blush as he looks at her and turn away, sure that he noticed, that he sees how she has become a woman (almost), even another (the other) woman in the house.

yes i tried to efface you, trace myself over you, wanting to be the one looked at, approved by male eyes. 'liked' was the word we

used. 'i think he likes you!' the signal of attention in the intricate game of the look during class, down the hall, on the field,
or, finely-timed, the walking home from school on opposite
sides of the street.

now i'm remembering. not dis- but re-membering. putting
things back together again, the things that have been split off,
set aside. what did it mean to leave behind that body aroused by
the feel of hot wind, ecstatic with the smell of sage, so excited i
could barely contain myself as we left pines and high-blue
eagle sky, and broke into the arid insect country of the
Okanagan with its jumping butterflies, its smell, familiar as
apricots, our mouths full of sweet pulp, bare legs sticky with it,
hot and itchy against each other, against the pelt of the dog, his
rank dogday smell as we rode the turns of the road down into
summer, real summer on our skin – do you remember? how
could you not?

we had endless photographs to remind us, you in baggy shorts
and blouse, dumping spoonfuls of canned mixed veg on our
plates ('Russian Salad for lunch!'), or you in peasant (there's
your word again) skirt and blouse, bandanna and hoop ear-
rings, like the gypsies you said we were, camping out. (you
wanted a caravan but all we had was the old blue Pontiac and
tents. you wanted a son but all you had were three daughters.)
the three of us in swimsuits, different ones each year, different
shapes and sizes of our growing bodies you presided over, our
father invisible behind the camera imaging moments of this
female world: eyes glowering with resentment, pudgy arms
crossed sullen in front, or else draped around each other, lithe
and smiling into tanned apparitions of ourselves. it's not *that* i
want to remember, how we looked or thought we ought to look,

learning so fast this other looked-at [*gaze*] image of ourselves. but how it felt to be alone unseen in the bushes of the canyon, pursuing those strange butterflies that folded themselves into grasshoppers whenever they stopped still. or lying face down in the dank smell of sand, unable to swim, hearing Jan and Marta's shouts splash into thin air, hearing wind rustle high in the cottonwood trees which did not bleed but, rooted to one spot, streamed into sky as i streamed too, feeling my dark insides, liquid now and leaving me, trickle into the sand – and i jumped up, scared, had i left a stain? would it show? the new worries being a woman meant.

i was slimming into another shape, finding a waist, gaining curves, attaining the sort of grace i was meant to have as a body marked *woman*'s. as if it were a brand name. as if there were a standard shape (as remote as the stars') to trim my individual lamp to, gain the stamp of approval for: 'feminine' translated a score of different ways: doll, chick, baby, kitten. diminished to the tyranny of eyes: 'was he looking at me?' 'did you see how he looked at you?'

boy-crazy you said, shaking your head as we drove, walked, rode obsessed past street corners, sauntered past certain spots on the beach, our heads full of advertising images, converting all action into the passive: to be seen.

'As you stand in Stanley Park (which was logged five times before 1889) you can almost hear the creaking of the yokes on the necks of the straining bulls, the rattle and clank of chains, the shout going up as a

*big log slews around on the skid-studded trail and noses into the bush
... the raucous bellow of the bullwhacker as he digs his goad into the
oxens' rumps:*

*Up Mack! Bright! Ham! By the jumped up devil that's in you, lean
into it! Moony! Blackie! By God – I'm comin'!'*

at night, when the woods no longer echo to the bull-puncher's
oaths, the rattle and grind of logs over skid trails has come to a
halt, the roar of belts, the scream of saws are finally stopped.
when the men playing cards by dim kerosene light are swap-
ping stories and hooch, adding up their time. when, in the set-
tlements, children shout a last gleeful game in the face of the
dark – then she sits writing:

'It is not that I am easily offended, as the older boys have soon
discovered – the "Lady-Teacher" can wield as firm a hand as
any Master. That which is wilful in me – the Devil's Grip as he
would call it – I may put to good use here.'

past two or three houses at the mill, someone walking up the
sawdust path glances into a lit room where a man, comfortably
seated, peruses an out-of-date paper, while his wife busies
herself with the children. or again, the onlooker sees a family
on its knees, the father with a Bible open in his hands, while the
children shift and peer and their mother, quietly devout,
kneels on.

'And I do smile now at Sheba's Paps, so discreetly clothed in

53

this weather. Yet sometimes a dark mood will take hold of me. I see that I am in the midst of freedom and yet not free, and could almost think how little is changed ...'

(is this familiar, Ina?)

in one of the cottages the onlooker sees a woman writing. he notes the fierce movement of her hand halted occasionally for thought, the absorbed air with which she bends her head to paper – a page, actually, of a book. he may think to himself, this woman is not writing a letter nor adding up figures, perhaps she is writing her own account of something that has befallen her, a history, say (though she is not exactly Moll Flanders).

'– and Rusty Pleece the worst of the lot. That ridiculous top hat – so battered the thing is almost green with mould, as well it might be. I do believe they spend more time warming their beards by Mr. Harvey's stove than earning a living. That I must walk past them each time to buy my provisions! That I must subject myself to the doffing of his hat and Evenin' Miz Teacher Ma'am – by which false courtesy he means to mock me. – I see it in the way they stare, with that rank odour of Liquor on them.'

Ana Richards preoccupied with the look the men give her. so many men and so few women in that place. with the benefit of hindsight (ah history, where all the threads of the story get woven out in their various entanglements), we know that Rusty Pleece ends up dying of smallpox in the contagious hospital on Deadman's Island. that drunk who got hauled in a wheelbarrow around Gastown saloons on Christmas Day, not merely a drunk, or not that only, dies in the hospital because he volunteers to nurse there.

a sense of fraternal community runs through the records. rivals and friends in business, in civic elections, setting their hands to great things: the establishment of law and order, of a post office, of a school, the celebration of the first Dominion Day.

'You would say, Father, they are a Rough Lot and this is no place for a Gentlewoman, and you would be right, perhaps. Still I would rather be here than cooped up there as your handmaiden.'

these few references to her father, from whom there never seem to be any letters or none that were preserved, betray a bitter relationship. no doubt overbearing, a clergyman with absolute authority as to the real (at least in his eyes), he must have been appalled at the thought of his daughter leaving him for the wilds of Canada. how did she manage to go against his express disapproval? did he cut her off, disallow her? she made her escape, with a certain amount of bitterness evident – 'handmaiden,' that Biblical word. with what shade of emotion did she choose it? 'a female personal attendant or servant.' personal? the object of whose hands? as in '... the relation between divines and handmaidens was a theme for endless jest.' yes, but who found it a laughing matter?

– now Annie, now you're indulging in outright speculation. this isn't history, it's pure invention.

– but what about the personal history of Mrs. Richards? (so personal it is hidden.) with what irony can we imagine her writing Mrs.?

– you're simply making things up, out of a perverse desire to obscure the truth.

55

whose truth, Ina? the truth is (your truth, my truth, if you would admit it) incest is always present, it's there in the way we're trained to solicit the look, and first of all the father's, Our Father's. framed by a phrase that judges (virgin / tramp), sized-up in a glance, objectified. that's what history offers, that's its allure, its pretence. 'history says of her ...' but when you're so framed, caught in the act, the (f) stop of act, fact – what recourse? step inside the picture and open it up.

logging photo caption: *Bull puncher and oxen relax momentarily, sullenly conscious of their ability to get any job done, no matter how tough.* the woodsman look. self-evident. the pose. as for the oxen?

*self-righteous*

there was the look you gave yourself, the look you looked (like) in the mirror. making up someone who was not you but some-one you might be. a desperate attempt to make up for the gap – between the way you actually looked in your blue dressing gown round and woolly in the mornings, your scrubbed shin-ing cheeks, anger in two humps between your brows, hair fine as a baby's wisping away in the rush of porridge-making – the gap between that and how you meant to look, how you ought to look, how you did as you clicked out the front door in a rush ('do up your coat! how many times do I have to tell you how slovenly you look?'), taking us with you in a panic to the doctor's, dentist's ('we're going to be late again!'), late but smartly dressed, high heels, tailored black coat, stylish hat with

*identity crisis*

its little veil. looking smart was part of your identity, evidence of the only job you had, not 'just a housewife' ('Canadian women have no pride – they look such frights on the street with their hair up in curlers'). caught between despair at being nothing ('just' a mother, 'just' a wife – faceless in, as you used to say, 'a thankless job') and the endless effort to live a lie (the loveable girl in her Lovable Bra, the Chanel femme fatale ...) how measure up?

you tried valiantly and for quite a long while. those mauve-blue stones, removed from the choker they were part of, sewn onto blue velvet – a ribbon, still a choker but soft, and soft your throat under it as i tied it for you, the dark blue of the velvet and the milky blue of the stones catching light from two pink lamps twinned and magnified in the mirror you were lost in – that hollow glance, that dark reflection of yourself seated at your dressing table in a cloud of daughters dazzled by the artistry of makeup, fragrance, the fractured light of jewels. the audience you played to, playing up the character of each: 'emeralds are your stone, darling, they bring out the colour of your eyes,' 'pearls are perfect for you, see how they glow against your skin.' rehearsing your will in the imagination of us fully grown, retelling the history of each piece, endowing us with its contin-uance, grandmother to mother to daughter, the female line of inheritance – 'these will be yours when i'm gone,' because that was all you had to give.

but i didn't understand that then, balked at, resisted the repeti-tion of your ending phrase, 'when I'm gone ...' as if you were soliciting pity. 'i don't want pearls, i want these.' 'oh Annie, you have no taste at all – that's just costume jewellery' (fancydress, masquerade). but it was that i wanted, that fake stone your real breath would mist in an instant – gone. elusive as your look.

57

was it only me who searched your eyes searching for you in the mirror you vanished from? powdering, every dab a small white lie, the brilliant reflection of no one i recognized. rosebud mouth, plucked brows, dark eyes intensified: the perfect implacable Garbo face. my fear began when i realized you never saw, as you turned away with a sudden frown or laugh, the you that was you, invisible in the mirror, look out at last.

implacable. (the exactly right stroke of the mascara brush.) incapable of appeasement. (hard to please, your own strictest judge of what was passable, erasing with cold cream and kleenex, beginning all over again.) not placable, not easily calmed or pacified (quick to be irritated at our presence, 'stop hanging over me.' nervous and late for a party you didn't want to attend. 'it's the Office Party,' you said, as if capital letters explained its necessity. and then, 'I only go for your father's sake.' and then, furiously wiping off your face, 'always knifing each other in the back, the hypocrites!')

*im-* not / *plak-* to be flat. layer, coating, floe (ice). flatfish, flake. to be calm (not). to please (not). placebo, placid, pleasant. none of these. a raging fire underneath, a tumult, sharp tongue, an inability to coat with sugar, please (dissemble), to fit in, no matter how you tried.

Zoe sitting across from me at the table, hunched in her black leather jacket, blowing the foam on her cappucino, fixes me with grave eyes: 'i distrust women who smile too much.' do i smile too much?

her gravity puzzles me. she's a visual artist of some kind, she speaks of 'commitment' and yet she is so secretive about what she does she tells me almost nothing about it. 'i use the city,' she said when i asked what her medium was. this stranger i happen to meet in the archives, thumbing her way through the photographs. we get talking and she wants to know all about my writing. why do you want to know? i ask. because you tell good stories, she says, and i wonder if she means i tell good lies, i cover up the way most women smile?

i'm feeling black, stuck. afraid to go further? i see my reflection in the window, head tilted as if bored, resting on one hand, elbow on the table, the other hand playing with a pen, playing at writing ... wondering (wandering?), wasting time. perhaps i lack commitment.

for here i am, thinking about being attractive. a middle-aged woman who hasn't held a job for twelve years. a middling woman muddling through as wife and mother. what have i done in all this time? (the small space a life gets boxed into.)

'he's such a wonderful prof, you must feel so lucky, Mrs. Anderson,' Richard's star student ('so bright') gushed at the last party, betraying herself. 'i do,' i said, i do, i do, with its eternal echo. the lie. the defensive lie our lying together is. the small space desire gets backed into. boxed. off.

want to?

(yes, no, yes) do *you*? (whoever initiates risks rejection, asks so as not to be asked, not to be tagged in the chronic game of blaming.)

you don't really want to, do you?

i do. it's you who doesn't (don't?).

if that's what you want to think ...

and we roll over into our individual silences. impasse. knowing neither of us really 'wants to' and neither of us will admit it.

– so you've made your bed, now lie in it.

– as you did, i suppose? and shall i try springs or foam or futon? move Richard out because he 'snores'? take hot milk, sleeping pills? your cures for all that frustrated energy you had no outlet for. confined to bed, to coffin, slowly mummifying.

– there you go, exaggerating again. you really must get yourself in hand.

– self-control, the by-word you threw out the window – bye to all that you inherited you'd push on me. a roundabout word for blocks and stops it wasn't control but repression they were after when they taught you that.

– what do you know about repression? you were hardly a virgin when you married, were you? i didn't know the first thing about sex – your grandmother simply refused to discuss it, though i begged her.

– the mothers, the inheritance of the mothers. you taught me a lot. you taught me the uneasy hole in myself and how to cover it up – cover girl, the great cover-story women inherit in fashion and makeup. you taught me how i was _supposed_ to look, the feminine act.

– i taught you to take pride in your appearance.

pride on the outside, and on the inside – shame. the taste of it in my mouth, musty as dirty linen and just as familial. sweaty socks in the laundry cupboard (ladies don't sweat), bloody panties. blood. the modess i was the first to use, in its blue box they'd wrap in plain paper at the drugstore. i was the first to get hairy. 'oooh, hair!' (they said it with envy as well as disgust, Jan and Marta.) i wanted to shave my legs like the other girls who stripped, lithe and clean-limbed for gym. you gave me a pumice stone. 'you're too young to shave.' i rubbed and rubbed but the hair never came off. 'your boobs jiggle,' said my best friend, 'why don't you get a bra?' 'don't be silly,' you said, 'you've hardly got anything there.' 'but Mom, all the girls have them, and they don't jiggle.' you opened my door one evening and handed me two collapsed things: 'you can use these old ones of mine. they shrank in the wash.' (these things that smelled of mother flesh, the used body, sagged on my spare frame like empty hammocks with a nipple fold embarrassing under sweaters.) 'i'll take in the seam,' you said.

take in the seam, make it seemly. make up the seeming okay. it wasn't. they flattened me like bandages.

wardrobes, wordrobes. 'you look perfectly all right, no one will ever notice' – those seamed bindings with the gone elastic. 'but they're uncomfortable.' 'brassieres are! (you called them brassy-ers – brassy hers? unconsciously, your judgement on them?) – what did you expect?' (you asked for it.) not _that_. i wanted bras like the other girls had, those soft white cups,

slightly padded, those round billows under a sweater. 'padded?
at your age! you've all got sex on the brain. how do they expect
you to learn anything at school when you're parading around
like that? we should have packed you off to England long ago.'
the great threat.

to repeat history. to put me through what you went through.
left for years at boarding school, even over the summer holi-
days, your parents off somewhere in India – did you wear bras
under your tunics and blazers? surely by age sixteen? did they
issue them along with the uniform? i never thought to ask who
initiated you. who bought you your first bra? and how it was
done.

the sins of the mothers. hating our bodies as if they had
betrayed us. but the words for our bodies betrayed us in the
very language we learned at school: 'cunt,' 'slit,' 'boob' ('you
boob, you dumb broad'). words betraying what the boys
thought of us. wounded or sick – 'you'll catch girl germs!' –
with a wound that bleeds over and over – 'on the rag again,' 'got
the curse,' 'falling off the roof.' catastrophic phrases we used
that equally betrayed us. handed down from friend to friend,
sister to sister, mother to daughter. hand-me-downs, too small
for what i really felt.

promise: the budding of some secret future in me, little knowing all the eggs were already there, lined up and waiting. promise: letting go, a rhythmically repeated event starting each
month from full. not a vessel waiting for someone to fill, but a
small storm, a slow flood subsiding on its own. 'vagina,' you
said was the word for that part of our bodies we had to keep
clean. we laughed together in the bathroom, Jan and Marta and
me. it sounded so royal, regina, vagina, so foreign a word for

something that was simply there, warm to touch, nice to rub, parting a little in the warmth of the bathtub. secretly looking it up in French i was astonished to discover it was masculine. le vagin. there must be some mistake, i thought, not knowing its history, a word for sheath, the cover of a sword. it wasn't a sword that i was promised.

*'In those days good timber was plentiful – good timber, on sea-coast slopes, that could be felled and shot right down to water – hand-loggers' timber. The country bristled with opportunities ...'*

*'Many a man I have heard lament those days. "Boys, oh boys!" one would say, "why was we all so slow in coming to this country? ... Why, anywhere round here all up the Inlets and round the islands there were the finest kinds of hand-logging shows. Why! the country hadn't been touched!"'*

touched ... felled and shot ... that isn't touching or even that other diminished one you used to use, 'so touching' (violets and tears) as if the male touch (topping and felling) required its polar opposite to right the world – split, split. and is it mad then, to talk to trees? and what is madness, Zoe?

promise, the excitement of it in the air, something wonderful or wild about to happen. i'd almost forgotten but for today, standing on the porch, my hands full of the flyers they keep leaving for no one to read – men with shabby bags full of the stuff, men who barely live on what they get paid, boys tossing words for extra spending money, pages and pages of words that slide in our front door and out the back, a trickle of waste – it wasn't that that was coming but the dark, the great overhanging dark that arrives with Hallowe'en, the dark of a storm gathering. it was all there: the same excitement rushing down the road to school, 'hurry, it's going to pour!' as it does, dark drops become a flood that drums through layers of leaves, the great horse chestnuts lining Windsor Road, hulls and nuts nestled under soggy leaves we wade our way through, ditch water swirling, water-mud smell of flood beginning its pour down a mountain side – and then the bright lights of school, the humid heat of wooden floors wet from boots, slickers, hats leaking small streams. warm and dry, we waited for the hurricane, at least that, huddled safe, preparing to be bored by the chatter of chalk, the sound of faded maps unrolling over the rain that was hurling itself at all the window panes. and it was *that* we listened to, and though we waited for it to happen, rain never broke the window, lightning never struck.

i stood on the porch and thought of us at school, of Harald intent in lit rooms of the Marine Building, totting up logging accounts, conferring with the other men, while you stood still in the house, a pile of clothes on one arm, apprehended in the sudden drumming of the rain. you were home, yes, home: walled in in the dark of the coast.

on such a night, say, when my sister Marta dreamt her endless dream of cougars stalking glow-eyed in the dark, what would Ana Richards think? puttering about her three rooms in shift and wrap, rechecking the fire banked down in the stove, plaiting her long hair into a braid for the night, slow to blow out the candle, thinking perhaps she should sit down, even at this hour, to mend her skirt – 'I have torn the skirt of my grey dress in a vain attempt to walk the shoreline to Granville' – at $40 a month she can ill-afford such scrapes. or worrying about the Miller boy, 'dull-witted and far too big for his boots,' wondering how to tell the Constable, that opinionated member of the School Board, that his son should be 'hefting his weight at the mill' instead of staring down the 'teacher-widder' at school. or thinking perhaps to add one further remark about the woman she has tried several times to describe, 'a soul attuned to the spirit of this place,' Mrs. Patterson, 'bonnetless and ignorant of the cedar bits in her hair,' singing with her girls on their way home from blackberry picking, or fired with righteous anger at the consequences of another liquor brawl – 'I could not bear to view the injuries she so valiantly attends. Would that i had her ~~courage~~!' crossed out and altered to 'strong-mindedness.'

Ana, lost in admiration, yet not lost, refuses to grant her courage, resists what she must have felt were Susan Patterson's too well-declared principles. or is she accurately assessing her own lack? prone to fantasizing, imagining what she has not experienced ( a 'born' writer perhaps), she lacks a certain proper sense of self. worries that she is too easily impressed, too easily invaded ... yet the invasions are real. a sudden rapping at her door, loud, imperious. at this hour what could it be but disaster? her chimney on fire? someone needing assistance? Mrs. Patterson perhaps? she almost knocks over her chair reaching for her shawl, remembers to shield the candle as she opens the door – onto darkness, obscure as black pall in the drumming rain. she hears feet thudding back up the trail, stifled laughter, someone shouts, 'Knockie Knockie, Run Awa'' and sees herself as she must be seen, caught in the doorway in nightclothes: Ginger Knocked Out.

Ana / Ina
whose story is this?


(the difference of a single letter)
(the sharing of a not)


she keeps insisting herself on the telling
because she was telling me right from the
beginning stories out of a life are stories,
true, true stories and real at once – this is
not a roman / ce, it doesn't deal with heroes

'A great "do" at the school tonight, being Addie P.'s birthday party, the outcome of two days worth of preparation, Mrs. P. having arranged matters to everyone's satisfaction. Yesterday she sent her Siwash woman, Ruth – that cannot be her real name – and the woman's mother, to scrub the Schoolhouse. As I was straightening books and the children's things, I observed Ruth to pass her fingers slowly over the slate, as if the letters marked thereon might leap into her very skin. Our Magic is different from theirs, I see – And yet it cannot capture them – the quiet with which each seems wrapt, a Grace ~~that~~ – the Grace of direct perception, surely, untroubled by letters, by mirrors, by some foolish notion of themselves such as we suffer from. I cannot find the words for this the others would dismiss as Pagan – perhaps our words cannot speak it.'

*religion*
*– environment*

\*

(pagan, if you only knew, Ana, goes back and right on through 'one who has no religion' – from an exclusively Christian point of view – to country-dweller, one who lives in a village surrounded by country, one who lives with country things which are not things but living creatures.)

\*

*FALSEHOOD OF THE HOUR: 'That Cotterell says the boys in camp are getting sick of bear meat. That a deputation is to wait on*

*Ike, begging him not to shoot more than 20 a week. That Ike will yield gracefully to their wishes ...'*

\*

*'Always bear in mind that boys are naturally wiser than you. Regard them as intellectual beings, who have access to certain sources of knowledge of which you are deprived, and seek to derive all the benefit you can from their peculiar attainments and experience.'*

\*

Lining up forks and spoons on either side of plates, she listened to the hum in the room, a different kind of hum from the usual suppressed wave of giggles, pokes, whispers, even the ritual drone of reading aloud. This was a purposeful hum, the swish of long skirts moving quickly, the tap of bootheels on wooden flooring, clink of dishes. Ruth and her mother moved serene on calloused feet, while Susan Patterson bustled, Jeannie Alexander lumbered with the extra weight of pregnancy. Perhaps I dance, Ana thought, smiling at the conceit, feeling light as the swaying paperchains. The door had been left open and a breeze trailed in, bringing with it, was it?, the early smell of spring, fresh green out there, longer light in the afternoon. Paperchains, English paperchains in a clearing in the bush – what was she remembering? Butter on a blue plate, Bridget's hands holding the butter bought from the farmer's wife that afternoon, butter and cream and strawberries and cake for her own birthday, eight or nine perhaps –

'Well!' Jeannie Alexander sighed, laying down the last napkin and straightening her back, 'do you recognize your schoolroom now, Mrs. Richards?'

It always surprised her, the Mrs., as if somebody had distorted her name. Mrs. Richards was her mother's name, had been. Once.

'It looks beautiful,' she said, eyeing the linen tablecloths (Mrs. Alexander's, brought from Scotland), the tureens, the ruby vase of ferns (Mrs. Patterson's, from America), the dowry things women brought with them, things from home. Things for making a new home, no matter where they found themselves at their husband's behest.

'I hope the children will be impressed,' she said, then bit her lip at the implied slur on their manners. These were their mothers, after all.

'Let's hope there are no accidents,' Susan Patterson agreed. 'It does look beautiful. A perfect place for a party.'

'I can't understand why we haven't used it before.'

'Yankee ingenuity, my dear!' Mrs. Patterson twirled on her heels with a snap of her fingers, the irrepressible in her that always took them by surprise, breaking through her grave exterior like sunshine.

Ruth looked puzzled. Ana clapped her hands. 'Oh wouldn't this make a splendid room for dancing?'

'Dancing!' Mrs. Alexander was shocked.

She had slipped, she a minister's daughter, still wearing the supposed weeds of widowhood, she the school teacher, a model of propriety no doubt – she who had danced once in her life on her escape from the confines of the rectory, her father's brooding dourness, 'dancing is the Devil's work, my child.' Dancing had led her mother astray, he said, her mother who had disappeared from their world, taking forever the gaiety his Christian forbearance refused to bear. 'Gone, Ana, she is dead for her sins.'

\*

*'Women in their course of action describe a smaller circle than men, but the perfection of a circle consists not in its dimensions, but in its correctness, says the logical Hannah More.'*

\*

'I cannot but think that I am failed somehow as a woman. Propriety I can, on the whole, master, but the patience, the strength of character, the unfailing sweetness and generosity of spirit you counselled, Father, all escape me. Perhaps I am the monster you feared I would become – Is it that I want what womanhood must content itself without?'

\*

'On Your Mark!' Captain Fry raised his right arm in the air, his left holding the pocketwatch, eyes fixed on the sweep of the second hand climbing up to twelve. Ana stood with the others

72

in front of the schoolhouse in the gathering dusk. The women had finished cleaning up the table. Ben Springer, just arrived with Mr. Alexander, stood at her elbow shaping the line: 'You there, the Siwash boy next to Addie Patterson, get your toe behind the mark, yes, *behind* it.' The mark was nothing but a toe scrape drawn with Richard Alexander's boot in packed sawdust. 'Spread down a bit there, Miller, that's right.'

'Get Set!' Captain Fry shouted. A light wind had started up as the day receded, she could smell dew in the sawdust, hear the trickle of water in the wooden flume. 'Hunker down, all of you!' Ben Springer advised as the boys were doing it, Ted Miller tossing aside his cap in a final grand gesture. The girls refused to 'hunker,' stood straight in long skirts and ribbons, except for Alice who, Ana noted, gripped her dress with small clenched fists and crouched.

'Go!' Captain Fry bellowed, and they were off. Puffs of dust behind flying heels, thud of booted feet down the path towards Mr. Alexander who stood staunchly in a line with the office gate, squaring himself against the rush of bodies flung around him and returning. She could hear him shout encouragement, and then 'No hanging on' as one of the boys used his body as a turning post. Caught up in the excitement, women and men alike shouted 'Come on! That's it!' encouraging the slow-pokes, the little ones by name, as the gap lengthened between a small knot at the front and those trailing behind. Alice was abreast of Ted Miller, her white eyelet lifted, stockinged legs flashing a quick tattoo, and then she had passed him, ribbons streaming, hair flying in the long moment of arrival, no one else ahead. And the frown of effort transformed, head high, free in her own momentum, she soared like a swan toward them. Ana saw it.

Ana's fascination:

the silence of trees
the silence of women

*ecofeminism*

if they could speak
an unconditioned language
what would they say?

when she let herself out of the house, it was night – it was moonlight and briars, it was the fascination of desire for what lay out of bounds. not Frankenstein, but the touch of the terrible, what she had only imagined her sister saw: God there in the burnt-out orchard in the woods. to come back and say she had seen Him, His scarred face with the scary eyes, His inhuman head, to touch and run back, home-free. it wasn't being jumped or the hands at her throat, it wasn't even the game (or that she was) – it was knowing where the real began, under the words that pretended something else.

and it wasn't God they were frightened of, or it was how He might reach them through her, their mother. they were afraid under the blood-red moon, a witches' moon, she said. she hugged her sister tight as they lay in bed together in the moonlight coming through her sister's room and discussed the probability of their mother's poisoning them in the food she so hated to cook. 'it's crazy to talk like this,' – 'but *she*'s crazy,' her sister said. their house was full of accident: peaches from the basement cupboard rife with botulism. contaminated meat. 'mother' in the vinegar. in the cupboard as if embalmed. a body, bodies somewhere.

she let herself out of the house because she wanted to see if she would be jumped, if He would lay his heavy hand upon her. she lay in a ditch, she walked for miles across the mountain, threw pebbles at her boyfriend's window. no answer. a kind cabbie drove her home for free, wrought up and weeping. 'someday you'll be happily married with kids and you won't even remember this.'

for years she had forgotten. but now half-hidden under pages of notes, under quotations from archival material, under sheets of xeroxed photographs (the facts), there is a scribbler on her table and the visible page reads: is it your fear, Ina, i hear in the rain falling all around the house? tonight the world seems shaky. i am filled with collapsing bridges, swallowed cars, dangling girders – why do i keep dreaming accidents? all these people standing on the span of a bridge which is slowly collapsing under their weight, my daughter falling in a long impossible arc into the water.

> *mother, may i go and bathe?*
> *yes, my darling daughter*

always there is the panic and the screaming, the lost bodies, my helplessness – always there is that. i can't seem to do anything. i can't warn her beforehand, i can't get through to help. always there is trouble with the phone. it is disconnected or the operator doesn't understand. we are thrown back on what we can't do in these situations. and who is we? we who warn:

> *but don't go near the water*

we who say 'yes, but' – who know the lure and the trap. who are daughter and mother, both. it is the world outside my door which looks at times insane and exceedingly dangerous. it is my own inability that is so dangerous. the worst is that we (that we again) have made it so. no, the worst is, we had no say in how it was made.

when Richard comes in for a cup of coffee and asks, well how's it going? i will mutter fine, shuffling maps and xeroxes to cover the scribbler. i have not found the courage yet, the honesty perhaps, to tell him i've lost interest in what he is doing. that my mind will no longer come to grips with lot numbers and survey maps, will no longer painstakingly piece together the picture he wants. faculty wife fails as research assistant fails as wife. that wasn't part of the original job description. come off it, as Ange would say with that beautiful longlipped sneer she has perfected, you *like* helping out, contributing to the Big Book, in which it is written: 'and to my wife without whose patient assistance this book would never have been completed.'

– the truth is, you want to tell you own story.

– and yours. ours. the truth is our stories are hidden from us by fear. your fear i inherited, mother dear.

– the truth is, that's woman's lot. it's what you learn to accept, like bleeding and hysterectomies, like intuition and dizzy spells – all the ways we don't fit into a man's world.

woman's lot, lot: an object used in making a determination or choice by chance (x and y, xx or xy and all that follows from that chance determination); a number of people or things ('fed up with the lot of you'); a piece of land (a lot too small for dogs and one mad Englishwoman); one's fortune in life; fate (predictable as the five potatoes to peel every day at five o'clock).

fate used to mean something promising and secret, something to do with stars and gypsy women who knew how to 'tell' them.

and if the sign in Burdett's Grocery announced 'This Clock is One Second Slow,' that was a joke on the others, people with deadlines (nervous and punctual at the dentist's office). we dallied reverently along the road, readers of bottlecaps and bubblegum comics. we were a whole economy trading in popsicle wrappers from the Black Cat cafe.

but the black cats plastered on the window next door, Cat's Paw, non-slip, for all walks of life – that we avoided. Bluebeard lurked inside, sullen as blacking, grim as the bottles hidden beneath his rags. buzz off! in the whine of mechanical brushes, in the odour of leather, laughter and fresh air died around us. from scavengers and traders we shrank into daughters with timid voices waiting on his pleasure to notice us at all. ('that dreadful man,' you said, 'i don't want you going in there alone.') we stood close to the door in twos, passed him the docket that was stained as the hand which took it back – and almost touched the stopped throats of wives, the stropped edge of razorblades.

was it you who named him? made up his story? or fixed him to one that was already waiting. it was you who refused to go in there, sending us off with the docket ('he's always sneering at me'). i didn't notice the pinch of the shoe as you squinched down into your 'lot,' your woman's lot – a little too small.

*'He went at every problem by the light of nature – "bald-headed," as the saying is – in furious attack. He would anchor out his wire cable around some tree, and make the donkey wind itself up mountain slopes, over rocks and stumps and windfall logs and all the obstacles of*

*newly-felled hillside forest. He would "jump the donk" aboard a raft from off the beach and tow it here and there along the coast ... He had no awe of his donkey, that great awkward mechanism, nor of its ailments. He used it as in earlier days he may have used a wheelbarrow, as a thing that could be trundled anywhere, with freedom.*

— *exploitation*

but what are you *doing*? i can imagine Richard saying, looking up from the pages with that expression with which he must confront his students over their papers: this doesn't go anywhere, you're just circling around the same idea – and all these bits and pieces thrown in – that's not how to use quotations.

irritated because i can't explain myself. just scribbling, i'll say. echoing your words, Ina – another quotation, except i quote myself (and what if our heads are full of other people's words? nothing *without* quotation marks.) *↳ story, ownership*

scribbler. scribbling. i look it up and it means writing. why do we think it so much less? because a child's scribble is unreadable? (she hasn't learned the codes, the quotes yet.) scribe is from the same root, *skeri*, to cut (the ties that bind us to something recognizable – the 'facts.') *↳ writing = violent?* *✳ ✳*

but this is nothing, i imagine him saying. meaning unreadable. because this nothing is a place he doesn't recognize, cut loose from history and its relentless progress towards some end. this is undefined territory, unaccountable. and so on edge.

from children maintaining a sugar economy we grew into somebody else's 'sugar,' 'honey.' we stopped scribbling and

*✳ cancer (Deb)*

started inking initials on our hands, our arms, on scraps of
paper, giving ourselves away. the new economy we traded in
was one based on the value of our bodies, and though we
couldn't have explained it (or accounted for ourselves within
it), we knew the rules the game was played by and we played it
to the hilt (o sheath, o vagin).

at Princess Pool, that pool made by damning up a mountain
creek – remote, good for illicit beer and wild laughter in the
bushes – we lay in the sun, tanning ourselves in the light of the
Look. we went there to be seen, to be certified Teen Angels,
Dolls. peering out of Adam's sleep, waiting to be Made (passive voice), we flaunted gorgeousness like second skin, expo-
sed in the noisy lure of rock ('chantilly lace, a pretty face'), the
flick of a cigarette ('that's what I like'), the slick of oil. 'don't
look at them,' Donna advised, 'just let them look,' as The
Hunks paraded by, eyeing the choice.

i looked at her instead, the soft rise of her breasts under her
suit, so much fuller than mine. i wondered if at home in bed
she ran her finger down between them, trying to deepen the
cleavage. i envied the gold blur of hair on her arms, her eyes
that laughed into mine as she leaned forward, her breasts
swinging with her: 'see that guy over by the board? isn't he
cute? he's been looking at us.' our slow walk to the water's edge
was ritual, stilted, forced. mirror images of ourselves, we posed
in the water, chatting aimlessly, unable to swim or really talk.

c'mon, i said, i'm tired of this. let's go to the other end – it's
beautiful there and it's shallow. and it was true, the reeds came
down the creek mouth in tall clumps we picked our way among,
halfhidden, wading deeper into the quiet, talking at last in our
own voices and with our own gestures. then we were swimming
and then you were flailing around, 'i can't touch bottom!' a few

82

short strokes and i'd grabbed you, yelling 'don't panic,' as you pulled me under, and we were both in a swirl of bubbles and water fighting each other, me thinking, we're going to drown, we're both going to drown, how stupid. i was angry at you for being so helpless, i was angry enough to fight you back to where we could stand. scared and white, 'you saved my life,' you said, 'i'll never forget.' and though i'd started to shake, i knew that wasn't really true. i had to, i said, you were pulling me under. but that was only part of it, because i can still remember the feel of your body as i fought you back, as i hugged you back to air.

and the will i felt. the sheer jubilation. i couldn't account for it then (i couldn't account for anything then).

*write her story!*

Ana, struggling to account for herself, writes: 'What is it I might say? I am well, praise God, the school is small and manageable. All the ladies here (there are ladies, Father, who keep an eye on me) have been most kind, as has Captain Raymur – Oh it conveys nothing, nothing of these sawdust byways ...'

*↳ language inadequate*

what has she left unsaid in those bracketed ladies keeping an eye on her? those anonymous ladies and then Captain Raymur, authoritative head of this small world. aloof, absorbed in the operations of the mill, he is merely the figure on whose authority livelihoods depend, including hers. and after his name, a break – in the line that is not hers, that she composes in imagination for her father's benefit. her real story begins where nothing is conveyed. where she cannot explain, describe –

'... this Rain that embraces everything ...'

*– language inadequate !*

i find it difficult to explain, Richard, what this scribbling means – and was there any way *she* could? laying down her pen and the

83

right word dancing in front of her eyes like some wisp, some
wing feather she must pluck from the air for him, for them,
their eyes waiting in rows in the empty room, waiting for her to
explain.


*'A one-room frame building, 18 x 40 feet, with a clapboard exterior
and cedar shake roof ...'*

his eyes staring from a vicarage window at wind-flattened
heath, waiting for her to explain

*'The building was provided with two 12-pane double sash windows
in each of three walls, wood stove at the back for heat, brass lamps on
wall brackets against the winter dark, fog or rain ...'*

imagine him holding her letter up towards the light with that
look on his face: [Ana, my wayward child, you are straying close
to animism, souls in trees and other pagan notions] you, the
daughter of a man of God. explain yourself.

*bad for woman to see this?*

*'Fifteen children were required by the provincial government to start
a school, and a family of Millers (6), Alexanders (2), two half-breed
children, a Kanaka boy who had jumped ship from Honolulu, and a
family of Pattersons (4) made up the magic number.'*

accounting for – the numbers must add up – but there was no
accounting for (nothing had prepared her for) these children of
millhands, loggers, and stevedores. children familiar with
eagles and bears, with killing accident, with salmonberry and
vanilla leaf. children who knew nothing of Blair's Sermons,
*The Young Lady's Friend,* or Shelley and Keats.

84

'I find myself in a new world, Father, and that has made all the difference.'

## Waking Up

Warm, wet ... she had given in to it, the slide into the pool ... brown water, yellow brown and flecked with leaves or green bits ... letting go ... Now she is awake, the feeling warm in her still, but seeping away, the secret pleasure of her body in its rooting place – who had she been with? There were others there on other paths, there had been a bear ...

H'yaa! Sukey shoo! A man's voice outside startled her. The pigs must be loose again. G'wan! She lay stiff under the quilt listening to their snorts and panicked trotters receding, and then the muffled sound of boots. She should have been up by now.

The mill had started with its clanking noise, and there was rain, she could tell by the wan light through the curtains. Sukey put the kettle on – reaching for her shawl and the chill, it was damp really, fringing up the sleeves of her nightdress. The stove would be stone cold.

As she crumpled up the paper, she crumpled news of a world beyond the clearing, beyond even New Westminster, head-lines of Russia and the Khanata of Khiva, pronouncements for Holloway's Ointment, Mara Villa Cocoa. There, it had caught, the lovely quick flame.

It was tea she needed, a good strong cup of the Darjeeling, and time, twenty minutes anyway, to set pen to paper. 'How the rain falls in this place – so thick you cannot imagine ...'

'You?' Why keep up the pretense? No one would ever follow that sentence. It was hers alone, leading her on. Down the trail of whatever it was had come, would come. Wet trees dripping in the dim, the almost unseen, almost indistinguishable track of other feet under hers, sensing their way along. There had been others, she thought she had seen Susan Patterson and her family, even the Alexanders, strolling through the trees, the men carrying picnic baskets, the women carrying children. And no one had seen her as she climbed between the ferns trying to find the path, interloper, almost ghost. No one had seen her as their paths diverged and she was lost, off the path, struggling through bushes, sure of the bear who seemed always to be following her – she broke through branches, stumbling on a pool, and found two women sitting there in the leafy water. Wisps of steam, warm, she knew it was warm. They beckoned to her. Rain fell warm around them, the brown water pulled at her skirts – it hadn't mattered, clothes fell away – she was about to change into something magical and sure ...

'Sure.' As the Americans say. Another world.

Time to enter it, you goose, she told herself. You had better go early enough to start a fire. Not that the day was really cold. It was the rain that made it seem so chill, sombre even, dripping off the firs. Woods and no words for them. Repeat after me:

> *With buds, and bells, and stars without a name,*
> *With all the gardener Fancy e'er could feign,*
> *Who breeding flowers, will never breed the same*

Not here at any rate.

not, not ... all these negatives knotted into the text. silent k. for what? kiss. xoxoxo in code. kisses and hugs. omitted. not in the letter of the law, not allowed in church. cuddling up close to you in your familiar black coat, i can smell the sweetness of your perfume and i'm bored, tired of the voice that drones on with its disapproving tone, its listening-to-itself sound that makes me not want to. sit up, you nudge me with your elbow, you're a big girl now, sit up. Harald sits on the other side of you, erect and serious, ignoring us. soon he will get up with the rest of the sidesmen to do his part, passing the collection platter down the aisle and then going up with the other men to offer it to the priest who offers it to God. i thrill with pride at my father standing so straight and handsome so close to heaven. Our Father. whom we ask to 'forgive us our trespassers' (those Burglars, Bogeymen, and Bad Boys). after all, property is nine-tenths of the law and trespassers will be prosecuted. i know that. i am ready to defend my father's kingdom (i have a place in it of course).

and then i learn that we are the trespassers, or rather that the trespasses without the *r* are ours, our sins, growing up wrong from the start.

girls wear hats and good dresses to church, you said, that's what your good dress is for. when you're old enough you can wear nylon stockings and garter belts, but from the first you wear hats. why do girls wear hats and boys don't? because women have to keep their heads covered in church. but why? they've always had to. but why? and then it comes out: the curse, the blood, the pangs of labour as the punishment for Eve's original sin.

87

i heard the spark of resentment in your voice. the spark that would flare into rage. rushing around, telling us to hurry up, getting yourself dressed up to the mark, smart (how did that become the mark of intelligence in women?), nerves at breaking point, and then some little thing ... you're hopeless, you never remember, you expect me to do everything, be your char, be your cook, and then look smart on top of it all, you set *out* to tee me off. look at you, going off to church as if butter wouldn't melt in your mouths, sitting there in that ridiculous pew for all the world like a Christian family, hypocrites, all of you, go on, put a good face on it, i'm going to bed ... hysteria.

hystery. the excision of women (who do not act but are acted upon). hysterectomy, the excision of wombs and ovaries by repression, by mechanical compression, by ice, by the knife. because we were 'wrong' from the start, our physiology faulty, preoccupied as we are with the things of the flesh. spiritless – except for our rages – 'going off the deep end' where the divers went. it was nothing so controlled as a dive, more like smashing into black waters where there were no limits to what could be said, no up nor down, no boundaries to respect, no real. always that seed of half-truth from which grew vast kelp beds of accusation. the harder i swam for the horizon line of the truth, the more insistently they curled around me, your truths: the neighbours criticizing you behind your back, 'bad wife, rotten mother,' the conspiracies of doctors out to cause you pain, to punish you for being a bad girl (gone bad – infected by your body). they removed your uterus, they pulled your rotten teeth, they put electrodes on your misbehaving brain. they would stop at nothing, including punishing your children to get at you, you said. and who was it who cut your fingers, burned your skin, kept you insomniac and cursing all the neighbours' dogs? either that or gone in a morning-after fog of sleeping pills. knock, knock. who's there?

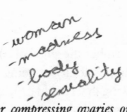

*'Mechanical devices were invented for compressing ovaries or for packing them in ice. In Germany, Hegar (1830-1914) and Friederich (1825-82) were using even more radical methods, including ovarectomy and cauterization of the clitoris. The source of hysteria was still, as in Plato's time, sought in the matrix of the female body, upon which surgical attacks were unleashed.'*

once there was a child with serious eyes and a delicate mouth, about to be sent away from home to boarding school. a child with soft hair cut straight around her ears, floppy white bow perched on her head, who sat on a carved chair clutching a teddy bear. her eyes looked straight out of the picture into some alien future, but they looked with a level gaze and steadily.

where did that child go?

that child, one with her body. not yet riven, not split into two – the self and the body that betrays the self. bleeding, leaking, growing lumps, getting pregnant, having abortions and miscarriages. all the bad timing, off days, things that weren't supposed to happen. 'female complaints,' in a hushed voice, 'women's trouble.' the body that defeats the self. *the* body, not even *your* body. split off, schizophrenic, suffering hysteric malfunction. all of this contained, unspoken, but sounded in the shame with which you handed me my first box of pads, showed me how to pin the ends to the tabs of a sanitary belt. adjust that bulky thing between my legs.

i remember the smell of crusted blood, the fear of it 'showing,' the impossibility of going swimming (all before tampons and knowing that i could do it anyway, that the bleeding would of its own accord slow down). now that i'm only a few years away from losing it altogether, i remember, despite all this, my secret pleasure, feeling the flow, a sudden rush of blood slide out between my lips and onto the pad. that quick loss of hearing in class, refocus of my self, from way out there with the coureurs de bois or x = what? to this inward trickle, this slow passage, intimate, and only from and for myself.

there is still even now the innate pleasure of seeing on a fresh white pad the first marks of red, bright red when the bleeding's at its peak. innate because of a childish astonishment, *i made that!* the mark of myself, my inscription in blood. i'm here. scribbling again.

⤷ *writing a place for oneself*

writing the period that arrives at no full stop. not the hand manipulating the pen. not the language of definition, of epoch and document, language explaining and justifying, but the words that flow out from within, running too quick to catch sometimes, at other times just an agonizingly slow trickle. the words of an interior history doesn't include ...

*language*

*history*

that erupts like a spring, like a wellspring of being, well-being inside ...

so write it that way then: Zoe.

brown eyes, brown, challenging me. perched behind her coffee cup, an air of ruffled insistence, persistent. 'you haven't even begun to think about what it would be if it could be what you want.' this. this to go on, this suspended time our table sits in, bare, our two sets of hands also in suspense beside these cups, half empty, cappucino wreaths around the rim, the corners of our lips, the faint taste of chocolate underlining it, our talk of Ana Richards, my disappointment in her fate, her *choice*, Zoe said, or maybe she didn't have any, i said. 'so what is it you want from her?' the question surrounds us sudden and floating, chairs suspended outside this ordinary cafe ...

## Naming

She heard herself, one hand on the child's slate, the other grasping the small brown hand with its bit of chalk, repeat for the third or fourth time, 'a for angel,' saying it in the hum of a class busy at copywork, in the smell of soap and dried mud and overheated skin squirming in its clothes – 'a for angel,' forcing the child's hand into an ellipse, drawing out the long a to match the curve of the letter, 'ā-ā-ā-n,' and then the straight stroke, '-gel, there's the wing, do you see?'

Lily's solemn face did not return her smile. Of course. What would she know of angels or English churches? Lily was not a name she'd have an image for – not the angelic white lilies of Easter at any rate. Small wild ones, dark ones, what did they call them? chocolate lilies, yes. a for angel was much too far-fetched. a for what then? aardvaark? Out of the ark, Ana, and off Ararat – *please*. There are other mountains, so many other unnamed mountains, right here.

The child pulled her hand back, her small body drawn into itself and coiled like a spring away from the teacher's desk, not touching it, not touching anything. She had felt Ana's impatience and was embarrassed. They were both embarrassed. There must be some other way of doing this, Ana thought again. [The letter with the sound, the sound with the word, but if the word doesn't mean anything, what then?]

— signifier/signified

'You pigshit!' There was the Miller boy shoving Lily's brother off his bench and Danny silently resisting. With one accord she was up, boot heels hitting the wooden floor in a clean rhythm of fury. 'Miller! I've warned you!'

'And I'm telling you, Ma'am, I'm not sitting next to any stinking halfbreed –' extricating his length from the schoolbench to face her. 'My dad says I don't have to neither, and he's a Trustee.' Her fury was turning cold and hard, like stone, like the stoniness of Danny's face turned the other way.

Is *that* what British Justice says? She would match power with power if he was going to play it that way. 'Let me tell you, Master Miller, the Government of this Colony declares that Siwash and Scot are both registered pupils of this school. Do I have to spell it out for you? I Will Respect My Fellow Pupils.' (I will not use a belt.) 'Fifty times please.' (As if it mattered. He was twice as big as she, boots and all, with a head to match.)

'Give it to *him*,' he sneered, 'he let the cruddy fart.' Bullying face flush with his own righteousness sneering down at her. Would she back down?

'That doesn't mean you can push him off his seat –' (that sounded weak, unauthoritative).

From the corner of her eye she glimpsed Lily and Danny and

the Kanaka boy intensely watching without appearing to do so. 'You have disturbed this school once too often, Miller. You may gather up your things and leave.' (What are you doing? Father on the school board. The Constable's red face with handlebar moustache, ex-logger, muttering expletives about her.)

'You can't do this,' he said, his voice faltering for once.

_____

you can't do this (as she is doing it), the voice of flouted authority, slightly panicked, sounding alarm as she goes right for the edge. over it and off the deep end. he is a lout and she has been playing chicken (there goes her job). no, he is a nuisance and she has saved her class. no, he is merely the all-too-readable signpost, End of her Rope / The Road – a limit she pushes past.

'that's the limit,' – you, striking out. times you'd rush out of the house screaming at us, jump into the car and back out, wheels spinning, tear along the Upper Levels past the limit, pushing your luck, outstripping the fury that breathed down your neck. we never knew if you'd come back. or thought we didn't. or knew, and hated the fear you put us through in the meantime. ('you won't appreciate me til i'm gone.') piecing the story together bit by bit, Harald coming to each of us in turn, what did you say to her? or we heard you slam out of the room where you'd been 'discussing,' his voice flat, trying to be calm, 'be sensible, Ina,' and yours on a rising note, 'there you go, sitting on the fence again so you can be above reproach and it's easy enough for you to say when i'm the one tormented by enemies

93

– oh yes, you can afford to be sensible, can't you?' bitch, we'd think, witch. how can he be so patient?

but he was – a saint, you used to say, a decent man, a father we should all be grateful for. we were.

 he was the one who brought us news of the world, the logging camps he flew to, the characters he encountered. Harald told us about the war (both the one he'd fought in and the cold one that surrounded us), gave us our pocket money, discussed our grades, asked if we knew what we wanted to be. he was the one who burned the trash each Saturday afternoon, burning the detritus of our life together (all those homework pages, all those sanitary pads) in great roaring flames that licked up towards the cedar. he was unafraid of fire, he was careful, he knew what he had to do.

why do i write of him only in the third person when it's you who's dead, Ina?

each day he braved the world to bring us money. 'poor man,' you sighed, staring at the lights of the city winking below us, 'rush hour must be terrible tonight.' he would be riding home in the Vauxhall with Jasper and Charles, the smoke from Jasper's pipe like incense around them as they quietly discussed the stock market and the latest federal budget.

occasionally we would pick him up at The Office after a shopping trip, The Office smelling of teak and paper, where we were introduced to his secretary. 'she's pretty isn't she?' you'd comment as he drove us home, hoping he would like the new dress that made you look slim, the hat that wasn't really extravagant.

he was the one you had to account for money to, in despair over balances and receipts. furious that it wouldn't 'come out right,' that he had to know where every penny went. and why couldn't he just write you another cheque if you were short? you always were. but when he wasn't obsessed with figures, stingy, and overbearing, he was patient to a fault, longsuffering, a saint.

you were terrified that he might die before you. 'what would I do,' you demanded, as if we could tell you, 'I don't know anything about taxes or banks.' neither did we. and we were grateful for him, the central pole of our world, backbone and head of the house we clung to – safe, you most of all.   → *father*

*marriage*

*'There is unanimous agreement that getting a husband – or in some cases a "protector" – is for her the most important of undertakings ... She will free herself from the parental home, from her mother's hold, she will open up her future, not by active conquest but by delivering herself up, passive and docile, into the hands of a new master.'*

## Walking to Gastown

As the timber began to thin against the light sky of the clearing and its noises grew more audible, hammering, dogs barking, voices hailing each other, she slowed her steps. Now she was at the last bend of the trail, steadying her feet on the two-plank walkway which was slippery with moss from months of rain. And now she was leaving it, she let the quiet grow around her, clung to it, letting go of the wariness that always gripped her when she walked this mile alone. What was she afraid of? Not the deer, who were as startled as she. Not bears or cougar – she had never seen them, though stories abounded. Madmen then? Drunken seamen, Indians running amok?

The millhands straggling by in groups of two or three were voluble and obsessed with their own jokes. They tipped their hats, saluted her, sometimes dug each other in the ribs. But a cold nod never failed to establish distance and they moved on. Once she had been frightened by the Indian crone they called the Virgin Mary, who had risen like an apparition out of bush, and joining the trail with her basket of shoots, roots, whatever they were, had given her a singularly flat look, a look not at her but through, as if she were a bush or fern. At first she had thought the old woman was blind, but no one blind could find the path like that. There had been a large amount of sky in those eyes. It was the look of mountains, when she could see them through fog and cloud, snowy otherwheres she had forgotten about until there they were suddenly on a clear day, perfectly present. She would like to know what those eyes saw.

And now, distinct, the smell of smoke and rubbish mixed with the rank smell of beach – tide must be out. As the forest smell receded she let go of the fern she had been weaving through her fingers – what would it be like to weave roots into baskets? What skill would it take of a different order? She checked her hands for tell-tale dust. Time to put on your gloves, Ana, look respectable. His behaviour has become a problem for the entire school – go on, rehearse it. Nervousness climbed her throat, blurring her sense of herself. She knew it would be best to speak first, air her grievance rather than wait for him to come to her with whatever exaggerated version Fred would tell. But how could she speak if even the words deserted her?

Remember it's a role, a part to play. *Mrs.* Richards, if you please. A woman of some authority, surely.

She paused at the edge and let herself be simply eyes, entranced all over again at the way low afternoon light embraced grey siding silvered by winters' worth of rain, or the occasional honey-coloured wood, raw, of new enterprise, the Provincial Government building (a cottage really) white-washed and stark, cabins fading among trees at the far edge. Her eyes were drawn to the double-storied hotels with their porticoes, verandahs even, standing in a ragged line fronting the shore. Wind shivered the waters but at low tide the Gran-ville Hotel wharf and Fernandes' float to his general store, a few dugout canoes alongside, were largely resting on muck.

Pulling her shawl tightly around her she picked her way past stumps and muddy spots to the maple, last of a grove so she had been told (Lucky-Lucky they said the Siwash called it, though the word meant something else) where they had beached their canoes, where Deighton had beached his all of seven years ago. The lone survivor of that grove, boxed in now with wooden planking, afforded a seat to several men in blankets who seemed to be waiting for something, outwaiting even the street which, with its wooden sidewalk erratic, disappearing into mud in places, looked merely temporary – a child's rocking horse on a nearby porch swaying slightly as if the child had just run off.

———————

leaving her parental home, 'she will open up her future,' as i dreamed of doing, from the frame of my bedroom window, past the dark conifers at night, the quiet blocks of houses closed for sleep, dreaming my future overtown in lights, city-brilliant across the harbour. a promise i was running to meet, uniquely mine and waiting to reveal itself to me. i wasn't dreaming of history, the already-made, but of making fresh tracks my own way (through the bush Ana strolls out of, into the light of a town-day, barely town, nothing but a coastal village then. liquor and merchandise and news.)

what did you dream, Ina, in your golfing skirt, demure knees, a pretty face they said at The Club, something immeasurably sad within those eyes. what did you imagine of a future so far away from your parents' house in the tropics, their dogs, their servants, their endless games of Ouija at the mahogany table, tipped-up sherry glasses gliding mysteriously under fingers' touch, letter by letter spelling out your fate: 'you will die insane in a foreign country.' you were already in a foreign country where you didn't belong. you had already been left in one, left at boarding school in a country they called 'home' which was nothing like the India you remembered. they left you there in England with strangers and brought you out to another foreign country, another army posting in the colonies. 'it wasn't real,' you said, 'that life.' real life had to do with bills and snow, with sawdust and fever thermometers and bargain clothes.

in your real life here – for this was the life you chose, opening up your future to it so your children wouldn't have to leave, so they could grow up in a country to which they belonged. in your real life here you scrubbed floors to *Swan Lake*, ironed sheets to *Les Sylphides*. day after short day, you had the rain and the dark trees for company. 'it gives me the willies,' you said.

what are the willies? i asked. young girls who died before they could be married, the record cover said, the Dance of the Wilis, girls who were only shades of themselves dancing in

98

white gowns in the depths of the forest. but why? they were victims of fate, you said.

fate. that path that led to marriage or death, no other fork in the trail. for once you decided to marry everything followed from that. 'just wait until you have children,' you said, and sometimes musingly, 'just think, if i'd married the dentist you wouldn't be here at all.'

one day you took me to see the Wilis. driving through the dark tunnel of the Park, its trees (unlogged, we thought) outlining on either side the narrow width of sky above, we came out by Lost Lagoon where the fountain danced its veils of colour falling like the stage-lit plumes of the Swan chorus, like the falling skirts of les Sylphides – magic, theatre, a new version of all the city held. i was being initiated into a world of middle-class romance. i was a girl, i had no defense. for months afterwards i dreamed of life as Canada's Fonteyn, aching to be supported, ethereal and tragic, in those muscled arms that held me aloft, transported.

– you always did want to be a 'star,' your name up in lights, admirers flocking to your door. you always wanted to be the centre of attention.

– what's wrong with wanting to be a hero? all children want it. Mickey wants to be Superman, Ange wants to be another pop star. she's updated the ballerina, that's all. i spent hours reading about Fonteyn, how 'in every role she sought the human heart.' it explained the rapture i felt when i saw her – i wanted to *be* her, to draw others out of themselves as she drew me. she didn't dance like a star, they said, she was 'just the medium through which the

99

music spoke.' you loved her too. why else did you take me to see her?

– dream, all dream. that's not what life's about, as you well know. look at you, much too gangly and tall for ballet. that's what they told you, wasn't it? i still remember how crushed you were. you have to make do with what you've got. and look at all you've got, two lovely children, a fine husband –

– you had three lovely children and a fine husband, were you happy?

– but that was my fault, that was the flaw in my character.

– and so you closed down, closed in on yourself, thinking it was all your fault – your solitude was retribution, wasn't it? the dreams and heroes gone, except the dream of perfect motherhood – impossible to live up to. but that you couldn't was your fault. and you had no friends to tell you otherwise.

– i had friends, but they were scattered elsewhere in more civilized parts of the world. people weren't friendly here.

– Claire was, she used to be your best friend.

– Claire Potts! we were never close. (and so you rewrite the script, erasing parts of it to keep your theme clear. a restricted meaning.)

i remember Claire who lived in the brown house on the corner

100

with its living room large enough for a Christmas pageant, parts for every kid on the block. i was the Virgin Mary. 'now *imagine,*' she stressed, 'you're a very pure young girl and you've just had a baby, a divine baby sent from God. your own body has given birth to this child which is on loan from God, your body has had *God* living in it in the form of a baby – now can you imagine the look on your face, a look of rapture, of wonder even!' after i got over the embarrassment of anyone talking so freely about being pregnant, i tried, i really tried. but it was like sitting for a photograph, my body constrained, modest and blushing (immodestly i thought about being pregnant and what that would feel like), the Wise Men and Shepherds bowing before me, the doll in my lap. all i could see was myself, my body present to the world, its sudden potential. i tried to find the 'human heart in the role,' or perhaps it was the inhuman heart – i tried very hard to look pure. after the clapping, after the mothers dispersed for tea and cookies, complimenting each other on their children's performances, walking up the road with you i said, 'well, what did you think?' 'you looked silly,' you said, 'with that sheet on your head and that soulful look on your face.'

were you jealous of Claire? her organizing a neighbourhood 'success'? her coaching your own daughter in motherhood? or was it one of those moments when you spoke the truth, something in you breaking free of fiction, the ideal, the false standard you and Claire and all the mothers were wrapped up in?

sometimes you saw so clearly i don't understand how you retreated into that other fiction.

## Walking in Gastown

Gaining the walk in front of Deighton House, she heard the hubbub inside, the clatter of glass, cigar smoke snaking out toward her as the doors opened to release three men deep in argument – 'they'll never bring 'er this far,' 'more sense to go with California, a damn sight closer ...'

'Well, well, and a blessed evenin' to *you*, Miss.' A stranger, a man she's not seen before (from New Westminster? from Moodyville across the inlet?) lighting up when he saw her as if she were a grouse flushed out of the bush, raising his hat with an extravagant gesture – mocking her, in fact, for being here at all. She gave him a curt nod and gazed across the street as if intent on buying meat at George Black's. Why should he make her feel she was trespassing?

Their voices dropped and she heard one comment, 'New school marm. Young for a widder, ain't she?' She flushed and crossed the street, angry at herself for blushing.

The men seated themselves on the Deighton House porch and resumed their discussion, while she was left with her resentment. That was the way it was. The man who had greeted her would be sitting with his elbows on his knees, leaning forward to make a point, oblivious to all but his idea. And if she glanced back to see if she had imagined him correctly, and if he happened to glance up then, that would be fatal, he would think she was interested in him.

She looked at George Black's shop and thought about buying a duck (you are here to see Constable Miller). She looked at George Black's bear, chained to his verandah (where will you begin to look for Miller? at the gaol?) and realized she was looking into small wild eyes. (Yes, she had seen a bear, she had forgotten this one.) Bears were said to be temperamental. You never knew when one would rear up from behind a bush and slash out at you. This one looked sad and rather mangy squatting in the refuse of its own droppings with a chain around its neck, its great claws negligent against the planking. The way it sat on its haunches it could have been a child sitting on the floor with imaginary blocks, invisible letters. Except that its eyes were the eyes of a beast – immeasurably sad. Why would a man keep a bear? It wasn't tame but dying.

(Have you lost all sense of yourself, all authority, all will power even? Make yourself go and find that Constable. What is a Constable but a logger in uniform? He doesn't even have a proper helmet. Just a title.)

She continued up the street, crossing again to the walkway now she was safely past Deighton's. Should she go and knock at the Miller cottage behind its picket fence? Encounter Mrs. Miller and possibly Fred? No, she wanted to avoid Fred until she had spoken to his father. Should she check at the gaol? the customs house? He might be chewing the fat, as they called it, with Tompkins Brew, that ineffectual man he had replaced who had been given the sinecure of customs officer. They said the only thing Brew did as constable was grow his beard several inches longer. The same would not be said of Miller who tended to be zealous in the pursuit of wrongdoers, even engaging in the occasional gun battle. (That didn't help. Really, Ana, you're hardly a criminal, even in his eyes. (In whose eyes then? whose?) You're an aggrieved school teacher, remember that. Remember that they need you here.)

Several men were leaving the Hole-in-the-Wall saloon. What if Miller were in there? Gathering information, say, or in the bar at the Granville Hotel? That would cause a stir if she went in there. Put him on the defensive. But then, on the other hand, it might be to her disadvantage since women never went in there, at least not ladies. Everything would stop and they would stare at her and what would she say in all that silence? But then what would it be like to be in there, listening in on their conversation? Something about the bars she had glimpsed through swinging doors – the white towels, the glasses stacked in shimmering pyramids, the amber liquor, an air of conviviality that seemed oddly familiar. She should have been born a man, she wanted too much. She wanted to be free or at least freer than she was, than she had managed to be. She wanted to know what it would be like to rent rooms in the Granville Hotel or the Deighton, buy a piano (passing ships had them sometimes), give music lessons and forget about answering to school trustees.

———————

Ana, what shall i make of you when you make of yourself more and more? now you want to give up your cottage at the mill, safely the school-marm's place, and live in a Gastown hotel, you who have scarcely sipped the red wine of communion. you are afraid, walking that trail through the bush in your grey poplin dress, respectable, your tiny boots, pulling your black shawl more tightly around you at the thought of bears, or men,

or even another woman gathering roots. you who cannot find the words to explain yourself, your sense of the real. you who literally cannot speak. though they speak about you, the men do, those others.   ~ language
~ voice

they write: 'It is not true that Leo. Harmon is a candidate for the "schoolmarm's" billet. That times would be lively round the school if he gets it ...' (did you know they were thinking of billeting you?) they write about each other too, men gossiping about men in 'Falsehoods of the Hour' – 'That the Constable is to have a scarlet and yellow uniform. That Miller feels "big" over the event' – a trickily labelled column in *The Moodyville Tickler*. the word of its anonymous editor ('No connection with the "China gentleman" upstairs') travels the round of shop counters, mill bunks, from Moodyville on the north shore to Hastings Mill and Gastown on the south. *The Tickler* with its ticklish (and touchy yes, requiring tactical handling) 'squibs,' to be taken in 'the same spirit that they are offered in, that of perfect good nature.' that the school marm least of all should take offence at perfect good nature, knowing what perfect is and good too. as for nature – he of course defines it, scarcely imagining that their natures might differ. this joke that chases her round the schoolhouse (and through the bush) of men's imagination, dodging truth with a Falsehood (Of The Hour) that doubles back to admit itself. a game, a small indulgence ('begging your pardon, Ma'am') at her expense, insists on what it disavows.

and so she stands there unsure which word to believe, the word that is only a joke or the word that is truth told in the guise of falsehood. only a joke in either case, and so dismissed, while she, she smarts under its real intent.

to speak what is disavowed. for that is where she is. in the gap
between two versions.

'*The barque* Whittier *carried a piano among its cabin furniture. The
master sold it to a Mrs. Schweppe, who resold it to Mrs. Richards,
and then the school teacher also gave piano lessons in her rooms in
Gastown.*'

or

'*Mrs. Schwappe (?) sold it to Mrs. Richards, school teacher, who
lived in a little three-room cottage back of the Hastings Sawmill
schoolhouse, and afterwards married Ben Springer.*'

– versions of truth / history

the gap, the fork between two roads so long ago – though one
was barely a road, a dirt road, not much bigger than a trail. i was
out for a walk with Donna, one of those Sunday walks before
dinner and studying. we'd escaped from the hotbed of home to
be out in the woods where we could exchange a shifting
currency of complaint, of hopes and fears, sensing our freedom before us, afraid to look, full of the difficulties of mothers,
of boyfriends at school. we came to a fork and saw one trail
blocked with a blue car. how did it get there? at first we thought
it abandoned but the window had steamed up and then we saw
two shapes on the back seat pulling apart. let's get out of here,
you said. did you see? i was intrigued, they were two women.
perverts, you replied, i feel sorry for them. we walked for some

time in silence. i thought about that leafy tunnel they'd chosen, the silence of dripping woods and, under glass as under water, two mouths meeting each other.

it wasn't sorrow you felt, or even pity – as if they had no choice. for they had chosen the woods, despite loggers, bears and God. i was struck by the daring of it: it wasn't a road one would easily drive down.

a fork in the road implies a choice, the will to choose. Ana, hesitating in the middle of her muddy road, wonders whether she wants to find Miller at all. to justify, to criticize with tact, to grovel with dignity for a job some say a man would handle better.

*'When women are among themselves, they don't speak at all as they do in a mixed situation. That's only an element of response.'*

for instance, as she pauses, not knowing which way to turn, there *is* this man, pleasant-faced, hat in hand, a flattering curiosity in his look, asking with solicitude if he might be of assistance. and it would be so easy to reply, to grant a smile, allow herself charmed by his wit, his valuing eye. as if fate were written there in large script for all to read.

but don't you think we read with a different eye? Zoe asks. like MR & MISS ILES, have you seen that one?

i know the street, the precise wall. like WE ARE A SIGN THAT ISN'T READ? and she is grinning.

the question is: will you let yourself be escorted home (you the passive grouse flushed from the bush) by this eager and voluble man on account of whom you will move your piano from the schoolhouse (or wherever it is) to a parlour in Moodyville, pleasing him, his friends, and later your children with occasional waltzes that dwindle slowly into silence through the years?

or will you manage to live in hotel rooms where you give lessons and become Gastown's first music teacher, solitary, skirting mud puddles on your own, a secret friend perhaps to Birdie Stewart, that other enterprising woman who, flying in the face of family and church, establishes her house that same year. Birdie in her sitting room, going over accounts, faces Ana with a frank glare: 'you'll never get beyond a cheap hotel on the mingy fees you make.' Bridie or Birdie with the wandering 'r' ('independent? faw! any one of my girls is more independent than you'), who will teach you how to drink and sing you vaudeville songs until you devise your own accompaniment, pick up the beat, laughing outright for the first time in years. ('now *there*'s a sparkle! there are songs in those hands of yours.') you admire her – admire – i always thought it had something to do with looking – you reflected differently in Birdie's eyes. you see yourself, or a part of yourself you hadn't known before. you admire this woman of caustic tongue with stories to tell, advice on how to survive] she causes you to smile (that's what it means) as you turn intrigued in the kerosene light (at the mill they use dogfish oil), fingering embroidered pillows from Frisco, japanned boxes, a bead-fringe shade, watching her invent with pleasure the exact sheen in its emerald jets by gasfire: 'now this, you see, is the green that says yes, like certain eyes. ah yes, i've seen them shine in rooms you can't even imagine, velvet paper, the best chairs – Capital Hill, my love, that's where i plan to be.'

'you can't even imagine'?

you turn intrigued, and your body turning in its long skirt, its fitted waist that hugs your hips, is caught in the act, you have caught yourself turning in Birdie's eyes. turning because of a spark, a gleam, your eyes are green (you had forgotten that) and you know them lit with the look of something you almost meet in Birdie's brown. you had not imagined – this

as history. unwritten.

come back, history calls, to the solid
ground of fact. you don't want to fall
off the edge of the world –

*TEA – No. 1 Congan, chests,*
  *OATMEAL – Robinson's, in tins,*
   *VINEGAR – In Bulk and case,*
    *PICKLES – Crosse and Blackwells,*
     *CURRANTS – in tins and barrels,*
      *CANDLES – Price's Belmont,*
       *CURRY POWDER, CAPERS, MUSTARD,*
        *VICTORIA SAUCE, SALAD OIL, in pts. and 1/2 pts.,*
         *SARDINES – 1/4 and 1/2 boxes.*

\*

'Tea at Mrs. A's with S., Mrs. A. very big with child. S. – I am so to call her, formality she said will not withstand the rigours of life in "the bush" – S. is forthright by nature and perhaps by Yankee custom. Then too she is midwife and nurse to so many with whom she is on intimate terms in life and death – How does she bear it? Mrs. A., chided for not taking her constitutional, said she had grown weary of being stared at. I understood perfectly but S. will not see what she does not want to see. Take it as tribute, my dear, she says. But that is not how they look.'

\*

to turn aside a look when it is the look of the agent (active) directed at (directing) the object of acquisition. to turn aside a look when it is the look of the man who prizes himself – Jamaica Ginger, Pains' Celery Compound, Buckingham's Dye for the Whiskers. the look of a man who has boarded ship (to leave the trace, the mark of his being there), who would see evidence everywhere of his power ...

*

FALSEHOOD OF THE HOUR: 'That Joe Gibson regulates the sun by the mill clock. That all three work together in perfect harmony ...'

*

They had finally settled in the glassed-in leanto on the west side of the house, as Susan Patterson had insisted. 'At least if I can't get you out for a walk, we can sit in the little porch where you can get some sun.' Amidst the cushions and the wooden seats, Jeannie Alexander in the rocker which Harriet, the Indian girl, moved out, along with the tea things Susan carried. 'For heaven's sake, I've lifted ailing men, I do believe I can carry a tea tray. Now you let Harriet take the rocker and Mrs. Richards arrange those cushions for you and I'll look after the tea.'

They settled themselves down, smoothing shawls, skirts – like so many hens settling our feathers, Ana thought. She felt unaccountably happy to sit with them in the sun and smell of wood and, faintly, roses. Roses? 'Ah, it's the petals from my Glasgow cutting,' Jeannie exclaimed. 'I gather them every year. D'ye catch their fragrance then?'

Harriet, waiting in the doorway, disappeared as cries issued from the two Alexander children somewhere inside (how directly she moves, Ana thought, she doesn't announce her coming or going at all).

Jeannie leaned back in her rocker with a tiny sigh, smiling under half-closed lids: 'What would I do without you, my dear? Things always seem right when you're here.'

But it's Harriet, Ana thought, who makes them right.

Susan went on pouring tea, sun glancing off the silver pot in a coin of light that slid along her lower jaw. 'Of course they are, my dear. And they will be.' Ana felt suddenly outside – they were speaking of something else.

\*

*'Mrs. John Peabody Patterson, née Emily Susan Branscombe ... a "Lady of Grace of St. John" in a wilderness of verdure ... a "Dame Hospitaller" alike to Indians and whites prior to hospitals and resident doctors.'*

\*

tea to be sipped, a saving grace. the reward of freight, lace at the cuff, backbone properly erect, extended on a silver plate a sigh (shared), small talk, small things in hand. conserves, preserves of energy lapped with the turning tide. to savour is to know how to pace, lacing fortitude and will with a temperate grace. each day she climbs the biological, floorboards ticking beneath her feet.

*

*FALSEHOOD OF THE HOUR: 'That Lockhart goes his pile on the "Annie Fraser" ... That Ike Johns has no objections to holding the stakes at a boat-race. That if he makes a bet and deposits his stakes but is unable to find his man after he has won, that the others may have some difficulty in finding theirs.'*

*

having tea as if. manners maketh woman, into lady – the lady-would-rather, that indirect thing a pose, a mode of offering, circuitous. figurehead, and having nothing. tea the liquid medium in which they breast the unspoken. going around in circles. claimed, unable to claim. boarded (up).

*

'Sure and he must be getting cramped in there, poor babe.' Jeannie smoothed her skirt down over her belly, fingers extended, wedding ring opulent and heavy on the swollen mound of her skirt. Ana felt permitted at last to stare – Jeannie all belly, preceded by it, as if by a monstrous assertion in the world. How could a woman's belly so transform itself?

No, she could not imagine the child, could only see that huge mass of flesh once an appropriate part of Jeannie now taking its own place as if it superceded her. She wanted to avert her gaze, yet she wanted to see, see what it would be like ... not from the outside (Jeannie gazing ruefully at Ana's pinched waist: 'As ye see, lass, coming on the bride ship does nothing for one's figure') but from the inside, what it would be like to let go, be this assertive flesh distended – beyond reason – pushing out to declare itself in the world.

*

*'As to whether he was the first white child on Burrard Inlet I cannot say, but he certainly was the first at Hastings Sawmill, because my mother not only confined Mrs. Alexander, but also afterwards nursed her. There were practically no white children born on Burrard Inlet; about the only births were Indian births; white women expecting confinement went to Victoria. You see, there was not a doctor nearer than New Westminster ...'*

*

teas. pickles. currants. ex Star of Jamaica. ex, out of

farflung reaches of the imperial mother, men exchanging goods, labelled the comforts of 'home,' for spars of wood, giant timbers struck from unknown territory. traffic (dealing) all this coming and going, this emptying and filling of ships' holds.

*

*'Mother was not a trained nurse, but she was a wonderful woman,*

*and Mrs. Alexander loved Mother and had great confidence in her,'* Alice Patterson remembers.

\*

loading, they sing out 'drop 'er there,' 'heave away,' 'let 'er go.' a pride of muscle, frame, handling all these female pronouns there in the theatre of history (see Progress, see Master of one's Destiny), a body armature that can be counted on, a body that doesn't secretly transform itself (from month to month) ...

\*

*'To the woman he said: I will greatly multiply your pain in child-bearing; in pain shall you bring forth children.'*

\*

the vessel she is – (full)filling her destiny.

\*

They were surrounded by trees at the edge of the clearing, she knew that. By the dark of standing timber, rain forest, and everywhere trees were cleared the rapid growth of bramble, salal, salmonberry thicket – 'bush.' But they were sitting with English china, Scotch shortbread, their talk dancing the leaf-dance shadow and light of weather, polite, of whether her time was near, Jeannie's aching back a sign, and Susan said, 'I'll

118

have a look at you after tea.' Ana saw her hand, that hand everything depended on, pressing deftly, pushing skilfully inside. Susan's hands that knew so much.

And even as she stopped there, Susan turned, addressing her with a smile: 'I understand Mr. Springer was much taken with your playing the other evening.'

Jeannie laughed. 'The Wit of Moodyville? The Sworn Bachelor himself? Dinna tell me the man has met his Match! Ah, my dear, we have few men as eligible as he.'

Ana made a slight grimace. 'He is not *my* match, let me assure you.'

'But surely,' Susan enquired, 'you plan to remarry? I cannot imagine a woman as good with children as you who would wish to remain childless.'

She looked down at her hands, which were not Susan's, and blushed, blushing further as she did so at the thought of how they would interpret it. He had meant her to think him attractive, she realized that when she looked up from her playing – tired, she had given herself to the music after supper, playing with an abandon the newly acquired piano roused in her, the slightly wistful pleasure of meeting old songs again so far from home, transported, all of them transported from other places, other memories – she glanced up to find him staring at her with the look of a man who had some sudden surmise. Bowing slightly, he had raised his glass to her and drained it. A frontier tribute she supposed, put off.

'I have no ...' she said, and stopped. Mrs. Alexander was lying back in her chair as if listening inwardly, hand on her belly, eyes closed. Susan put down her cup. 'My dear!'

Jeannie Alexander opened her eyes on a room, Ana saw, that had faded slightly and smiled. 'He seems to have decided it's time.'

*

the only extant photograph of the Alexanders' first house is dated 1890 and shows a woodframe bungalow with glassed-in leanto on one end, possibly used as a sunporch. the photographer stood outside the picket fence and shot from the corner where the leanto begins. you can see the shake roof, the two brick chimneys, a large creeper climbing the wall to the peak of the roof – too tall to be a rose, even a rambling rose (even seventeen years old?). running down the length of the house in front is an open porch with five men wearing business suits and posing on or by the railing in various attitudes for posterity (prosperity). the caption reads: 'Hastings Sawmill. First dwelling of R.H. Alexander, afterwards manager. Later occupied by office men as bachelors hall ...' followed by a list of their names. and where is Jeannie Alexander in all this?

*

'I expected her groaning – pain and sorrow, the Biblical words, the pangs of which they speak. I expected the rending apart of flesh, the blood – now I write of it Biblically but that is not how it was. What words are there? I expected the screaming most of all, because that is what I remember when I heard how Mother suffered behind the closed door ...'

*

*FALSEHOOD OF THE HOUR: 'That Philander is "down" on the "Pearl." That he has any reason to be ...'*

*

the ships men ride into the pages of history. the winning names. the nameless women who are vessels of their destiny. the ship R.H., H.O. ride into history as stars on board the mute matter of being wife and mother – ahistoric, muddled in the mundane, incessantly repeating, their names 'writ in water.'

*

After the flurry of things to be attended to – Harriet and hot water, the children upset by a sense of crisis, the bed remade, Jeannie was helped out of her wet dress, the birth pad found – now there was quiet and waiting. Now there was the apprehension Ana felt staring through a bedroom window at the evening light, amber and viscous as honey. She let her eyes bathe in it, trying to feel it embrace her. Susan had glanced up only a moment ago and she realized she was tapping on the glass in nervous staccato. Rebuked, she looked out.

'The snares of death compassed me round about ...' Round

121

about were the shining sides of mill shacks, the shining of water, of distant trees in the smoky air. Mountains and mountains round about.

But Jeannie was oblivious to such thoughts. Head back on the pillow, knees up, she was breathing hard, concentrating all of her being on the upheaval within. Ana wondered at this transformation of the woman who had entertained them over tea. Her social charm, the small talk of her station, had disappeared, leaving an elemental creature, sweat beading her face, hair pushed back by Susan's patient hand, mouth open panting with pain – was it pain?

'... and the pains of hell gat hold of me.'

She had not cried out, not yet. Perhaps she would not. Susan's assurance filled the room. She sat by the bed, calm, encouraging, murmuring information in the quiet moments – Mr. Alexander had had his supper, Harriet would stay the night, everything was proceeding as it should. Proceeding, Ana thought, under full sail we are proceeding through the gates of hell.

*

*WHY THE "PEARL" LOST! Some say the "Annie Fraser" is the better boat. Others, again, will tell you that the "Pearl" is the best boat. But that the "Annie Fraser" had the better crew. Some go further and say that the "Pearl" is the boat and had the best crew, but that luck or the current was against them ...'*

*

the rattling of paper news his mental ticker-tape of what is worthy of attention (or diversionary, small artificial columns of another world), the quiet seeping of a light into the room, familiar as milky tea the drawing of a pipe – all these diversionary, turn the traffic of the mind around a gaping hole, this entry  *gaps* into or exit from – (blank, blank) – us here ongoing, playing by the rules

\*

She should sit down on the other side of the bed and take Jeannie's hand – she could see how tightly Susan's was clenched. But something kept her at the window, on edge. Was it Mr. Alexander's brief visit? His hearty entrance into the room (meant to reassure them?), his parting comment that these things were best left to women. She had felt his underlying discomfort, unease even. She saw how Jeannie struggled up to reassure him. As if it were he who needed attention. But what right had she to make such judgements? This was his bedroom she, almost a stranger, stood in, this was his marriage bed in which his child had been conceived. And she was a woman who knew nothing about such things. But she *was* a woman, and she was with women doing women's work.

Turning again into the darkening room, she saw Jeannie's knees spread, as if afloat in the white sheet, and Susan quietly bent between them looking for a sign. She felt a wave of admiration for these women joined in a singular work together. It was a rite, an ancient place she had been admitted to, this crossing over into life. A child, yes, a child was coming – not a death, a loss. And she was meant to share in it. *life!*

Pulling up a chair, she sat by the bed and carefully touched Jeannie's hand. There was an answering clasp, though the eyes did not open, nor the face break its concentration. She glanced at Susan who nodded reassuringly as the next wave came, a growing pressure on her hand, a driven panting breath, contracted into a groan – the sheer work of giant muscle moving underneath the sheet. Susan wiped her friend's brow with a cloth and Jeannie's eyes fluttered open, questioning. 'You're doing beautifully, my dear.' Ana settled into her chair.

*

*'It is, as a general thing, a rule in these cases that the first boat to pass the Judge wins – in fact, the one which comes in first. This was to be the rule, too, in the race on Dominion Day. But as the "Annie Fraser" came in first, the "Pearl" could not do more than come in second, unless she "tied." Well she came in second, and was consequently beaten; while the "Annie Fraser" came in first, and consequently won. That is really the true solution of the whole matter."*

*

reason, atomizing the question into consecutive parts, in order, by measure, establishes rule and precedent, coming first, establishing its rule over 'chance.' impartial reason. stock of the bystander. 'after the fact,' that is, at a safe distance (after fistfights, after the drunken disputes of the partial.) a 'true solution' logic says is the way it happens so it must happen thus. happening (by rule) to have this problem: that worth be established by competition.

*

woman a rhythm in touch with her body its tides coming in not first nor last nor lost <u>she circles back on herself</u> repeats her breathing out and in two heartbeats here not winning or losing labouring into the manifest.

*

'I had never before seen a woman's body truly at work. – Not *labour* as we commonly use it – I mean its <u>inner work</u>, this bringing forth. The pains were hard enough to break her, I feared. But she was not only at <u>their mercy</u>, she was labouring *with* them ...'

*

out and in. <u>out *and* in.</u>  – *cyclic?*

*

'Now bear down and PUSH, my dear, PUSH!' There was an urgency in Susan's voice and Ana peered, holding the oil lamp high enough to give them light, trying to see past Susan's head bent between the spread thighs. Before them, Harriet crouched by the bed, supporting Jeannie's shoulders, face calm, watching them.

Ana caught a glimpse of dark almost purple flesh and stood up, shocked. How dark it looked, an angry powerful o, stretched, stretched, hair springing black above. <u>This was Jeannie, this was something else not Jeannie, not anyone, this was a mouth working its own inarticulate urge, opening deep</u> –  *birth*

'The crown! Can you see it?' Susan looked up, elated. 'The babe's just crowned. Now Jeannie, now, PUSH – now not so hard –' And Ana was saying Push, even as she caught a glimpse of what she almost failed to recognize: a massive syllable of slippery flesh slide out the open mouth. Susan's hands were there, wet and streaked with blood, and a child was in them, moving its limbs and stretching its tiny mouth to cry – a male child, tied to its origin within by a blue twisting cord. Strenuous with sudden air, it uttered a squall of protest. 'Just as you thought,' Susan laughed, 'a boy.'

*

'I must confess I was taken aback by the babe's equipment – So large they seemed on such a tiny creature. Perhaps I had expected a girl, or had not thought much either way. What did I expect? This secret space between our limbs we keep so hidden – is yet so, what? What words are there? If *it* could speak! – As indeed it did: it spoke the babe, and then the afterbirth, a *voice* bleeding mass of meat. I was watching it begin to close when Susan covered her up.'

*

mouth speaking flesh. she touches it to make it tell her present in this other language so difficult to translate. the difference.

the caption could have read: 'Hastings Sawmill. House of Jeannie Alexander, first white mother.' but there were other mothers there, Susan Patterson for one. it was the event of this birth, the coming into place: 'Site of first white birthing at

Kum-kum-lee,' the point having no English geographic name, no transplant label, before 'Hastings Sawmill.'

to be born in, enter from birth that place (that shoreline place of scarlet maples, since cut down) with no known name – see it, risen in waves, these scarlet leaves, lips all bleeding into the air, given (birth), given in greeting, the given surrounds him now. surrounds her, her country she has come into, the country of her body.

to be there from the first. indigene. *ingenuus* (born in), native, natural, free(born) – at home from the beginning.

\*

*– body*
*– belonging*
*– nature*
*– freedom*

she longed for it.

worlds apart she says
the world is


a-historic
she who is you
or me
          'i'
address this to

- woman
- history
- bodies

the real history of women, Zoe says, is unwritten because it runs through our bodies: we give birth to each other. she is hunched over her cappucino in her secondhand leather jacket that makes her look small. she sits with her shoulders hunched forward, slightly aggressive (don't mess with me), slightly protective of what is tender in her.

but we give birth to men too.

no, we don't, she says, we give birth to boy babies and men make men of them as fast as they can. they try to make us think they make women of us too but it's not true. it's women imagining all that women could be that brings us into the world.

you talk about imagining, i argue – i always want to argue with Zoe – but what has that got to do with our bodies?

she sucks up the froth on her cappucino, eyeing me over the rim of her cup. as she sets it down she says, sometimes I think you like to play dumb.

like you like to play esoteric, i snap back without even thinking. she makes a face at me and laughs. only then can i admit she's right (though i'm right about her too). i think of Jeannie's birthing and what Ana saw – not the 'first white child born on Burrard Inlet' but a woman's body in its intimacy, giving birth.

we give it and it is unwritten because it is given, she muses. like all of women's domestic labour. like all of yours except this book.

she is my first, my ongoing reader. you, i want to say. but you are not reading this as i write and Ina is – in my imagination, Ina i would give birth to, enter her into the world. but it is Zoe's hand that rests beside mine on the table top. she sits facing me in the cafe, perches on her chair like a small animal, self-contained. offers me her attention, all of it, speaks fiercely – as if she were used to fighting her way through the world, or through the thicket of others' definitions she resists. i think of Ange and think that she is, in some way, like her. that shifts me suddenly, i feel old, as if i were talking to a woman so much younger. no, as if i see myself through her eyes – stuck in the unspoken, unenacted – half born.

she catches the thought flit across my face, asks gently, what is it? and i know why i'm here.

here, Ina, in a way you couldn't be. wandering around the empty house of your body, sleeping pills in hand.

'past history,' i say, quoting that phrase i've heard Ange use. as if we could emphasize it into the ground: PAST (its epitaph). but it keeps passing me by, with a nod between the lines.

she touches the back of my hand. that's the trouble with history – it never is.

we talk about the last century when scientists first established that women had eggs equally necessary to the making of a baby. how, before that, they saw the womb as a sort of compost

heap waiting to nourish the man's 'seed' which already contained a minute and perfectly-formed human being. we talk
about woman seen as soil(ed), base matter, material without
soul (air), or at least a soul so opaque, so burdened with men's
need, it barely has strength to rise. we talk about what Ange is
going through, what we went through, in the language of a different period: the development of women's alienation from
their bodies, suppressed hysteria, the 'wandering,' the absent
womb. and how it surfaces:

*woman – body*
*– surfaces / depths*

*'(Her body) is a burden: worn away in service to the species, bleeding
each month, proliferating passively, it is not for her a pure instrument
for getting a grip on the world but an opaque physical presence; it is no
certain source of pleasure and it creates lacerating pains; it contains
menaces; woman feels endangered by her "insides".'*

a woman of your generation wrote that, Ina, in a country where
birth control was illegal, but i think it was true for you too, to
some extent for all of us. perhaps that explains why our writing,
which we also live inside of, is different from men's, and not a
tool, not a 'pure instrument for getting a grip on the world.' 'it
contains menaces,' traps, pitfalls – i stop at the word 'our' and
think of yours, how it hurts to think of your 'scribblings' under
the bed (the bed!) in a language which was not yours. 'laughter
is the best medicine.' 'grin and bear it.' those bannerheads you
tried to muster to: woman's valiancy. trying to shape up.

133

we let you go into the hands of the doctors who 'punished' you for not shaping up. they said you suffered from delusions, said you were paranoid, said they were doing what they did for your own good.

perhaps they said Ben Springer was a good man too. told her women needed protection, told her about the bears, the drunken sailors, Indians running amok. said these things were facts, or facts of life she ought to be aware of here on the coast. (nobody used the word taboo, nobody mentioned garrison mentality.)

history is built on a groundwork of fact, Richard states. Richard is a good historian, known for the diligent research behind his books. one missing piece can change the shape of the whole picture – you see how important your part in it is? but i'm no longer doing my part looking for missing pieces. at least not missing facts. not when there are missing persons in all this rubble.

history married her to Ben Springer and wrote her off.

wrote her *in*, Zoe insists, listed her as belonging.

entered as Mrs., she enters his house as his wife. she has no first name, she has no place, no place on the street, not if she's a 'good woman.' her writing stops.

but what about Birdie Stewart? what about that other life in a Gastown room? and who was Mrs. Richards Mrs. to? Birdie is laughing, her magnificent head thrown back, hair glinting red in the lamplight, glass still cocked in the air – 'to the Missus!' she says, and breaks up at her own joke. 'you're no more a widow than i am, love. admit it. you've wanted to make your own way in the world, to come and go as you please. but you're afraid, my dear, afraid of your own twat.'

Ana is shocked – no, i'm shocked. just as i was when Zoe suggested their relationship the other day. what other alternative would she have had? lifting her shoulders in that characteristic gesture. you want her to have the consciousness we have, but what would she have done with it in 1873? → *has much changed?*

but this is a monstrous leap of imagination, i protest. (whose voice is that?)

so be monstrous then, she says.

but the monster is always someone / something else. the real monster is fear, or the monster is what i always feared as real: the violence behind the kiss, the brutal hand beneath the surgical glove, the one who punishes you for seeing (through) him.

that's your voice, Ina, lucid and critical, seeing through the conventions that surrounded you. and though you saw through them, you still didn't know what to do with the fear that found you alone on the far side of where you were 'supposed' to be. wrong, therefore. guilty of 'going to far.' (in the woods alone.)

they said you were disturbed, Ina, as if you were a nest whose eggs had been removed (they had), or as if our nest, the house, had been fingered over, picked through by some strange force from outside. electric, the rage in you. sitting on the stairs, my arm around Jan to comfort her (it was me i comforted), we listened to you shout at Harald white-hot words. it wasn't what you said but the fury of your speech, it wasn't speech but pure venting, a torrent repeated over and over. i thought you would kill him, i thought you would take the miniature kris he used to open letters, neatly slitting them down the side as opposed to your thumb-torn edges – i thought you would throw the pewter cigarette-case, vacuum-sealed from the tropics – i thought you would tear the hinges off his intricate chinese desk, scatter his careful accounts to the wind – you didn't.

time like a wind drove you, all the things you had to do, and he was so slow, so careful not to hurt. now i know the pressure that drove you against the balance of his approach, sagacious, carefully reasoned ('fence-sitter,' you screamed). you needed someone to knock holes in the walls instead of showing you, calmly, how the doors worked if only you would oil them properly.

*trapped*

for it was the walls that closed in on you, picture windows that never opened, doors that stayed shut against the cold. none of the openness of that stone house in the tropics with its verandahs and archways through which people came and went, all kinds of people, dogs, bats and cheechas running in and out. we exchanged this for Canada and lost our place in the tropics, which was not truly ours and where we had no rightful place. Tuan, Mem, and Missee times three – colonial children holding power over adults who were our servants but seemed more like us, wily as us at circumventing rules, at keeping us mum with horror stories and illicit treats, while the governors, Tuan and Mem, remained benevolent and remote, a small model of the government of the state, this house in which we took our place, when we could, on the side of the servants, on the side of secret trespassing, though we knew it was no side, that they too would punish us on command. while you negotiated the cross-currents of Mother and Mem, organizing a world

*identity negotiation*

around the Tuan who entered tired from the heat and the office, this sanctuary of flowers, of polished mahogany, of graceful light shining along the stone tile (hubbub confined to the kitchen). hours of music and drinks, watching the sun set in the strait. 'this magic world.' nights of dinner parties, *piht* parties, dances at the Club. 'it can't last.' wishing you had more time to spend with the children, suspecting Amah of undermining your position, of weaning our affection from you, worrying about your place in it all.

you never lived alone. you went from your parents' colonial house to boarding school, then back to your parents and into marriage with your own servants. always you lived surrounded by voices: quarrels, dreams, demands, the crises of others in several different languages. you never lived alone until you came here and found yourself suddenly placed with empty days on your hands, weeks and months of days alone in a house with all its chores crying out for you to do. the voices came from inside now, the way you whipped yourself into a frenzy of activity in the face of nothing. 'getting things done.' the never-ending round of them while we were off in school and Harald across the harbour in his office. you were always home where your place was, with the sawdust furnace, with the wood stove for heat, hanging clothes anywhere you could to dry them. filling up the silence with songs. black working songs, slave songs. 'Ol' Man River,' 'Lazy-bones' – always the question: 'how you gonna git yo' day's work done?' when it is never done, never over with, and there is no one there to witness your accomplishment.

perhaps i've been writing this as a bedtime story for you, Ina – surely now it's my turn. but you've drifted off into another world, and i'm left here telling, untelling, unravelling all the stories, faltering to a stop ... how should this one end? and is there one? (yours hasn't ended with you.)

*- cyclic?*
*- connection*

## Not a Bad End

Sitting on the horsehair sofa in Birdie's room, she is turning her glass around in her hands, watching the lamplight catch in its fluted base (these crassly ornate glasses, where did Birdie bring them from? what city? what companionship she cannot imagine?) Yes, she is shocked, but that only demonstrates the confines of her class and culture. She is getting used to feeling shock as the sensation of a door opening inside her. But she had never thought of herself as afraid: constrained yes, apprehensive yes, doing what was expected of her, simply because it was a way of biding her time until she could act. She had come out to the colony, hadn't she? and on her own 'steam,' as Birdie would say. But that wasn't enough. What if biding one's time could stretch into forever?

She knows, without glancing up, that Birdie is watching her with an amused expression. In Birdie's eyes she is all too transparent. It's not, surely, that she's afraid of her own sex? Or is she? And what, then, would being unafraid feel like? It is her turn to speak but the longer she reflects the more difficult it is to find anything to say. She thinks suddenly, I could not bear to lose this coming here, this room so full of ornate things that reflect the weather of her moods, this room full of her perfume and the sound of her skirt, this room ... as if the room were all she could bear to consider, not daring to lift her eyes to the woman herself who ...

There is a decisive sound of Birdie's glass being set upon the table, the rustle of poplin across the carpet, and the sinking-rising bounce of the sofa as she settles beside her. There is her warmth and the solidity of her body. Still Ana can not look up.

'You fear what you want.' Birdie's hand cups her chin and turns it gently towards her, 'am I right, my love?'

Lifting her eyes in a sudden rush of desire she reads likewise in Birdie's face, a sudden rush of relief – 'You see it written across my face,' she admits.

———

Ana, what are you doing? under the guise of such formality, you've moved beyond what i can tell of you, you've taken the leap into this new possibility and i can't imagine what you would say.

which means history wins again?

as if it were a race – one wins, the other has to lose. like the weather lady swinging on her platform, like the blue Virgin swinging on the other end of her polarity with the Scarlet Woman: when i'm out, you're in. but what if they balance each other (it's one of those half-cloudy, half-sunny days) and we live in history *and* imagination.

but once history's onstage, histrionic as usual (all those wars, all those historic judgements), the a-historic hasn't a speaking part. what's imagination next to the weight of the (f)actual?

well, you could say you've imagined your way into what she really wants, Zoe says, staring into her cup. is that where it ends? she seems distant today, preoccupied. i want to ask why but we've never exchanged much about our personal lives. i don't even know her closest friends. people she knows come in to the cafe, not that she greets them – though the odd one will stop by our table – but she feels them come in, i've come to recognize it in her, as if a muscle twitched, as if there were some subtle shift in her body. (another form of history she doesn't fill me in on.) she goes on talking, we go on talking, and the aura of her intensity surrounds our table like a mauve shadow, a certain light, neon, the others do not cross.

today the light is fainter, dimmer than usual. is it something i've said? perhaps she's tired of the story.

i suppose i'm getting near the end, i offer. it's just that i don't know what to do with them.

it's *your* novel, she says.

but that's the trouble with characters ...

'characters.' you talk as if they were strangers. who are they if they aren't you?

that's too easy. (something in me is irritated.) you know that Mrs. Richards was a historical personage, we've talked about how she appears in the records, and Mrs. Alexander, and Birdie Stewart, and Susan Patterson. (i'm beginning to sound like Richard.) they all existed, they all really lived. i owe them something.

-reread- keeping 140

truth, i suppose? fidelity? she sneers. as if you were *impersonating* them. there is that fierce cold look in her face – and you? do you really exist?

the cafe we are sitting in together has fallen away.

we're in some deadfall i'm struggling through – she's sprung a joke, but no, she's serious. she hates this fiction i've been forcing on her, is tired now of being its only reader, of being only a reader-in. she's shifted ground without warning. turned the tables. and i recognize Ina in that phrase.

no, you're not just a role, a robe i put on, one of your long evening gowns with the coffee-coloured beads, the shimmering sequins you had no use for here. you're not the empty dress of some character hanging on the line. you go on living in me, catching me out. my fear, my critic:

– i thought you were telling a story.

– 'impersonating' you? if i'm telling a story i'm untelling it. untelling the real. trying to get back the child who went too far, got lost in the woods, walked into the arms of Frankenstein –

– you mean that Spanish movie about a child's fantasy? it was only a fantasy, and anyway she almost died.

– but she didn't! she lived. remember that scene where he comes upon her in the woods and she shows him how to float flowers in the river? she tries to befriend him and later she tries to save the actual man.

141

– but he didn't live, remember? the man she thought was Frankenstein gets killed in the end. that's the trouble . with Frankenstein – you have to kill him before he kills you.

– actually Frankenstein was the man who created him. did you ever read the book? <u>and now we call the monster by his name. a man's name for man's fear of the wild, the uncontrolled. that's where *she* lives</u>.

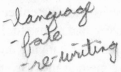

– well i always thought it was a morbid story. and to think a woman wrote it! still you can't rewrite what's been written.

– like fate?

– yes. the writing on the wall.

no wonder you were afraid. sick with the <u>fear of fate</u>, you walked in a world of disasters. the house would burn down while you were out shopping, your child would be abducted, raped (you wept the whole evening i was gone on my first date), Harald was late because he had been killed in a traffic accident – not to mention the ongoing, the newsboy who hit the door each morning just to wake you, the milkman who refused to understand your notes, the teachers who deliberately harrassed us just to 'take us down a peg or two.' deliberately was your favourite word, as if the world were full of those who deliberated against you in a struggle for control, theirs over you. the torment was that these things might be avoided if you could exercise some control yourself – if only you hadn't, or if only you could ... fatal errors, mistakes, lack of judgement that brought huge consequences. it was the intimacy of fate that shattered you, the way it worked close in to your life, that face-less power that had to be named, blamed on someone you knew. because i don't remember you worrying about the larger doom, about bomb shelters and escape routes, though every-one talked about them and the papers ran feature articles on what we were supposed to do if the Russians Dropped the Bomb. at school we practised fire drills and dropped our heads on the desk with our arms folded over them. at home we read the Sunday Comics and learned that there were communist infiltrators all around us. if it happens it happens, you said, let's hope it's a direct hit. while i worried about whether we'd have to leave the dog, how we'd get around the lineup on the high-way and what would we do when the road petered out in the mountains?

you wanted it to end, the world i mean, at least the world as it was then constituted. because for you there was no way out. we felt your wanting it and it scared us, Jan and me (Marta was too young), as we stayed up late, whispering in bed together, wondering about the peaches you'd fed us for dessert (botu-lism! you said, if one of us got a stomach ache), the chicken we'd had (it must have been off, you said). would you deliber-ately put an end to us, we wondered.

that was under the lemon moon of spring when i was sixteen and longing to escape the house, to bike long distances at night, dance, drink, sit in my boyfriend's car at the drive-in where the others were, explore the larger world of night with its noisy gathering places, its dangers, its illicit pleasures. that was the time of agonized waiting by the telephone, afraid of being left out, of being uninvited to the Great Party whirling by outside –

_—alienation_ 143

no, that was the time when Harald worried over what to do with you, when he came to my bedroom and we had long discussions about depression and what the psychiatrist said. you could go into hospital for only a few days, for treatment that would erase the thoughts that tormented you, and then you'd be yourself again in a week or two.

yourself again: who was that? i could barely remember the mother who'd laughed at 'Hokey-Pokey,' loved Abbott and Costello, read 'The King asked the Queen and the Queen asked the Dairy-Maid' in funny voices ...

*'Glissando in Electric Shock Therapy is the method of applying the shock stimulus to the patient in a smooth, gradually increasing manner so that the severity of the initial onset is minimized.'*

the mother who devised gypsy costumes for backyard plays, hid Easter eggs in unimaginable places, drove us hysterical with giggles impersonating the Ladies' Auxilliary ...

*'Glissando rate of rise, variable from .4 seconds to 2.0 seconds in steps of 0.2 second may be selected to regulate the degree of "glide" into the actual shock treatment.'*

taught us the winds, bamboos, and flowers, tapped spirits with a tipped-up sherry glass, constructed boats from the silver paper of chocolate bars ...

we outgrew all of that. left it behind.

*'The patient is clearly identified as the "sick" member of the family and the family is reassured they don't need to feel guilty or in any way responsible.'*

when Harald brought you back from the hospital he brought back a stranger, a small round person collapsed in on herself, who drifted in her blue dressing-gown in a fog from table to window to bed as if nothing looked familiar, as if home were a motel they had stuck you in with some people you vaguely knew. he said you'd had a difficult time and we must be good and do as much as we could around the house until you got better.

*'In the amnesia caused by all electric shocks, the level of the whole intellect is lowered ...'*

Ana's pen is poised, but she has stopped writing. there seems to be nothing to write at this point but the inevitable end of the sentence moving as it does toward the period and stasis. 'Today I have accepted ...'

no, no.

what if that life should close in on her like the lid of a hope chest? if she should shrivel and die inside, constricted by the narrow range of what was acceptable for Mrs. Springer? if all the other selves she might be were erased – secret diarist, pioneer pianist, travelling companion to Birdie Stewart – unvalidated, unacceptable, in short. because they weren't the right words. try artist, try explorer – prefaced always by lady, no, it wasn't a choice anyone sane would make.

to fly in the face of common sense, social convention, ethics – the weight of history. to fly ...

*'The stronger the amnesia, the more severe the underlying brain cell damage must be.'*

taking out the dead wood. pruning back the unproductive. it was all a matter of husbandry, 'the careful management of resources.' for everybody's good, of course. a matter of course. (by definition.) *ecofeminism*.

that fiction, that lie that you can't change the ending! it's already pre-ordained, prescribed – just what the doctor ordered – in the incontrovertible logic of cause and effect.

and the body gone off, into some fleshless realm where it is neither meet (met) nor right. in the delicacy of our lying together at night, two crystal sets still playing the old tunes under the covers, Richard touches me gingerly and mainly because he feels he ought to. i inch closer in a gesture that could be interpreted as comfort-seeking. he slides his arm under my neck and gives a little sigh. well that was a good night's work, he says, wasn't it? you seemed busy. so did you, i retort. neither of us wants to be the tired reason not to. his left hand lies on my belly, lightly, trying not to betray consequence. you know, i've been thinking about this book of yours – his left hand sliding down – i didn't exactly encourage it at first ('encourage'?) but i think it's a good thing. his fingers playing absent-mindedly. i didn't want to lose a good research assistant – pure selfishness, you know. but you're right, it's time you did something on your own. and i can always train one of my grad students to replace you.

'replace you.' and there i am, tugging at the cord that binds, filled with dread at the thought. dying to offer my time again, so as not to be left out of the book, the marriage, history.

> *you put your left hand in*
> *you take you left hand out*

or sitting hunched over the kitchen table, struggling with what

comes next in the gap thought doesn't leap, i look up to find
Ange in the door, observing me. what a space case! (the beautiful mask of her face made up for the world.) you've gotten as
bad as Dad. how come you never have fun anymore?

and i have to say all the limiting things: no later than midnight,
no going downtown.

fun? i think, and look it up as if it were a foreign word. having
fun. doing it for fun. in fun (sometimes). making fun of – here it
turns. to trick, make fun of. fool someone. from *fon, fonne* (feminine?), a fool.

un-fooling myself then. turning things around.

> *you put your whole self in*
> *you take your whole self out*
> *you put your whole self in*
> *and you shake it all about*

turning yourself around in the pokey, the magic circle we
stepped inside of, that hokey pokey, the family that holds
together at the expense of one.

when Harald brought you home, he brought home a new fear
(who's there?) that no one was there at all. Mum: mum. wandering around in some lost place, incapable of saying what it
was they'd done to you. under the role or robe was no one. certainly mother was gone because, in the damage they had done,
you had barely the energy to look after yourself. the you that
was you curled up like a small animal inside. lost in the harm
(for which there was no reparation, ever). they erased whole
parts of you, shocked them out, overloaded the circuits so you

couldn't bear to remember. re-member. you went looking for something, someone, rummaging in cupboards where fear stood up and you couldn't put those fantom limbs together into a shape by which you recognized yourself. that shape walking through time towards you. obliterated in a neural explosion.

*'It was something like science fiction. I was alive. I could feel. I felt as if I could think. But the fuel of thinking wasn't there. And it didn't come back.'*

cooking, shopping, driving the car: everything seemed difficult and huge. i hovered beside you, addressed you as if i were your mother, dressed you in rags of patience, comfort, trying to make them fit as i repeated what the doctor told Harald, that it was only temporary, soon it would all come back. everything i said was a lie.

for there you were, walking evidence of what you'd claimed, that the doctors were in league to get you. they'd got you all right. oh not your wispy hair, your pink cheeks shiny without makeup, your crooked teeth you wouldn't smile for. it was more insidious than that. your eyes were empty, flat, your shoulders sagged.

you'd gone flat, like a balloon at the end of the party. it wasn't just your memory they took. they took your imagination, your will to create things differently.

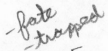
– fate
– trapped

and so you went on, [a character flattened by destiny, caught between the covers of a book[

i don't want to do that to you. i don't want Ana to do that to herself.

(there goes Annie, assuming she's different from each of them. safe in her parentheses, her own cover story. conservatively smug and untouched. meanwhile dreaming bridges that collapse, her daughter drowning, her husband's body thrown into the sea as the ship of state blows up, as the fire begins and she is swimming, swimming to save herself ...

break the parentheses and let it all surface! falling apart. we are( i am) we have fallen apart. the parts don't fit. not well. never whole. never did.

Zoe!

which is not the end. the story is 'only a story' insofar as it ends.

in life we go on. i call her on the phone. Zoe – I just want to say her name, as if that might solve everything, but she is waiting there on the other end, waiting to hear what i have to say in all this silence humming between us on the line – a line that is no line, that doesn't stop. Zoe, i don't know how to end it, i don't even think i want to.

she gives me her address, tells me to come.

it is an old house in the East End, a house that is layered with people's lives, a history of cooking smells, of mildewed wood, dream-soaked walls. she shared it with two other women (i hadn't imagined ...). Eunice and Zoe were talking at the kitchen table while they folded and applied stamps to a pile of flyers (i hadn't imagined her working ...) Zoe cut her sponge in half so i could join them. Norah came back with four cappucinos from a cafe down the street and we sat together, hundreds of tiny images of the Queen passing under my thumb, music i'd never heard running under the sound of their voices, so used to each other, half-phrases, jokes, retorts, half-silence when the words spun on inside our heads – 'our' in body, i was there too, listening to the play of it, though i didn't say much, i wanted to listen, as i used to listen in the woods to the quiet interplay of wind, trees, rain, creeping things under the leaves – this world of connection:

Zoe with friends in the kitchen they share, their shared life on the walls, posters, photos, notes, dried flowers. Zoe who was Zoe and more, at ease, at home, keeping an eye out for me in the strangeness of it all – the names i didn't know, singers, organizers, acronyms of committees, events i'd never heard of she was living inside – and yet observing too. quick to laugh, quick to object. Eunice so breezy in manner, full of the crisis centre where she works. Norah small and efficient. all of us absorbed in that kitchen where the flyers piled higher, the coffee cups grew cold and well-licked, the music quieter.

what did you expect? Zoe asked as we stood at the door. she had come outside with me into the dark.

nothing (sliding over the inadmissible, a dark river) – I couldn't imagine the place you would live in.

there were trees, there was a moon. and everything seemed to hang on my words that were sliding away from what they wanted.

Annie – she said, as if it were fiction, as if there were quotation marks around it – Annie Richards. the sound of a door closing.

i want to knock: can you hear? i want to answer her who's there? not Ana or Ina, those transparent covers. Ana Richards Richard's Anna. fooling myself on the other side of history as if it were a line dividing the real from the unreal. Annie / Ana – arose by any other name, whole wardrobes of names guarding the limitations – we rise above them. Annie isn't Richard's or even Springer's.

Annie Torrent, i said. (she looked up from the water she was floating something on in the dark, white robes or words, silver boats.)

so, Annie Torrent – she took my hand – what is it you want?

she asks me to present myself, to take the leap, as the blood rushes into my face and i can speak: you. i want you. *and* me. together.

she isn't surprised. it isn't even Frankenstein but a nameless part i know. terror has to do with the trembling that takes you out of yourself. we go up the stairs, we enter a room that is alive with the smell of her. bleeding and soft. her on my tongue. she trembles violently on my lips.

we give place, giving words, giving birth, to
each other – she and me. you. hot skin writing
skin. fluid edge, wick, wick. she draws me
out. you she breathes, is where we meet.
breeze from the window reaching you now, trees
out there, streets you might walk down, will,
soon. it isn't dark but the luxury of being
has woken you, the reach of your desire, reading
us into the page ahead.

# Daphne Marlatt

Vancouver writer Daphne Marlatt has published thirteen
books of poetry and / or prose in Canada and the U.S.,
written a historical drama for CBC, and edited two books
of oral history for the BC Provincial Archives. In addition
she co-edited, with several others, the proceedings of the
1983 Women and Words / Les femmes et les mots
conference in Vancouver, *In The Feminine.* She has also
co-edited several little magazines (*The Capilano Review,
periodics, Island*) and is a founding member of the editorial
collective *tessera* which publishes Québecoise and
English-Canadian feminist criticism and writing.

# Books by Daphne Marlatt

POETRY

*leaf leaf / s*, Los Angeles: Black Sparrow Press, 1969
*Vancouver Poems*, Toronto: Coach House Press, 1972
*Steveston*, Vancouver: Talonbooks, 1972 and Edmonton:
Longspoon Press, 1984, with photographs
by Robert Minden
*Selected Writing: Net Work*, Vancouver:
Talonbooks, 1980, edited by Fred Wah
*here & there*, Lantzville, BC: Island Writing Series, 1981
*mauve* and *character*, Montreal: Nouvelle barre du jour /
Writing, 1985, 1986, in translation with Nicole Brossard
*double negative*, Charlottetown, PEI: Gynergy Books, 1988,
with Betsy Warland

POEM / NARRATIVES

*Frames of a Story*, Toronto: Ryerson Press, 1968
*Rings*, Vancouver: Vancouver Community Press, 1971
*Our Lives*, Carrboro, NC: Truck Press, 1975 and
Lantzville, BC: Oolichan Press, 1980
*The Story, She Said*, Vancouver: BC Monthly Press, 1977,
with George Bowering, Brian Fawcett, Dwight Gardiner,
Gladys Hindmarch, Gerry Gilbert,
Carole Itter, Roy Kiyooka
*What Matters: Writing 1968-70*, Toronto:
Coach House Press, 1980
*How Hug a Stone*, Winnipeg: Turnstone Press, 1983
*Touch to my Tongue*, Edmonton: Longspoon Press, 1984,
with photographs by Cheryl Sourkes

NOVELS

*Zócalo*, Toronto: Coach House Press, 1977
*Ana Historic*, Toronto: Coach House Press, 1988

# Acknowledgements

thanks to Betsy Warland, Jane Rule, Helen Sonthoff,
Sandy Duncan, Sheila Watson, George Bowering.
particular thanks to Michael Ondaatje.

grateful appreciation to the Vancouver City Archives, the
Historic Photos Division of the Vancouver Public Library,
and the Ontario Arts Council.

parts of this novel have appeared in *Writing, The Malahat
Review, The Capilano Review, Canadian Forum*
and *West Coast Review.*

I would like to thank the following sources who provided
much help in the writing of this book:
Ralph Andrews, *Glory Days of Logging* (Superior
Publishing, 1956); Simone de Beauvoir, *The Second Sex*
(Bantam, 1952); Leonard Roy Frank, *The History of Shock
Treatment* (Frank, 1978); M. Allerdale Grainger,
*Woodsmen of the West* (1964; used by permission of the
Canadian Publishers, McClelland and Stewart, Toronto);
James Hillman, *The Myth of Analysis* (Harper, 1978); J.S.
Matthews, *Early Vancouver* (Vancouver City Archives,
1932); Alan Morley, *Vancouver: From Milltown to
Metropolis* (Mitchell Press, 1961); A.M. Ross, 'The
Romance of Vancouver's First Schools,' in James M.
Sandison, *Schools of Old Vancouver* (Vancouver Historical
Society, 1971); M. Watson and R.W. Young, *A History
and Geography of British Columbia* (Gage, 1906); early
newspapers, *The Moodyville Tickler* (1878)
and *The Mainland Guardian* (1873).

this is a work of fiction; historical personages have been
fictionalized to possible and / or purely imaginary lengths.

- signifier/signified → language = inadequate
  ↳ how do we tell our stories

ecofeminism!

- Canadian authors
- environmentalism vs. literature
- need literature to write/carve a place/
  identity for ourselves
- logging as erasure → but need trees for
  paper in order to write + fight erasure
    ↳ oral history/cultures
      ↳ diff. kind of literacy
        → can't survive?

- memory erasure → Obasan, Van Wyck
- nature in Atwood's Surfacing
    ↳ videotaping    - also ecofeminism...

- need to tear down history just as Marlatt
  tore down the road?

- does Canada need to write its story as
  much as women do?
    ↳ sense of anonymity, overshadowing?